MAKE OR BREAK IN MARRAKESH

IAN PARSON

This book is dedicated to all those searching for love

CHAPTER ONE

Justin Tondidori was thirty-nine years old. He was slightly overweight, his hairline was receding, and he was on a mission to be in a relationship before these issues grew worse. Before he hit middle age.

He was shallow enough to believe that if you were to stand any chance of finding a girlfriend you had to meet certain expectations, so he played the role he thought women looked for in a man, rather than being himself.

He thought the phrase 'just be yourself' was a trap.

Most days he dressed the same way he had since he was fifteen, in that grungy style made popular in the nineties by Kurt Cobain. Worse than dressing like a child, he still daydreamed like a child. Justin dreamed of being loved.

It was all he wanted in the world.

He knew his parents loved him and probably his sister too. That wasn't the love he yearned after. They were his family. They sort of had no choice.

He wanted the other kind of love. The unconditional, all-encompassing, take your breath away kind. Like in the movies.

Justin had seen *Love Story,* and he wanted that.

Many years had passed, and still he was hoping that one day it would happen. So far, he hadn't even liked anyone enough to experienced missing them when they weren't around. Nor had he ever known how it felt to put someone else's interests ahead of his own without an ulterior motive.

Being the childish romantic that he was, he thought this wasn't fair, he felt left out. As though he was lacking something, a key ingredient without which his adult life hadn't properly started yet.

He had nearly reached the tender age of forty, and still that elusive state of happiness eluded him. Some might say he was old enough to know better. That it was time to put childish dreams away.

Yet the idea of what true love should be. What it must feel like, what he was missing out on, had always ached within him. If he gave up on that what was the point of anything?

Over the years, Justin had taken many lovers and watched plenty of porn. He saw these things as part of a training regime, preparing him for the big event. Consequently, he'd learnt something about the physical expression of love.

Unfortunately, he'd failed completely to realise this wasn't enough. That he also needed to get in touch with his feelings, his emotions.

This was a department in which he showed no maturity. Emotionally his growth was stunted. He was no better than a clueless schoolboy, aimlessly searching for love's impossible dream.

After each fresh failure he'd lick his wounds and tell himself, *'She just wasn't the one'* or *'I tried, I really tried.'*

Playing the victim nullified any need to examine if he might be, in some small way, partly to blame for the latest failed relationship.

Without the necessary soul searching, he could genuinely convince himself that he was trying his best. The way his brain performed somersaults to reach such conclusions would have been adorable if the consequences weren't so tragic.

A large part of Justin's problem is that he thinks on the dating scale, he's a seven-and-a-half at least, probably an eight.

Arguably there was a brief moment he was eightish. But that was years ago. He's nearly forty now, his best days are far behind him. He's a six-and-a-half at best.

Despite that, in his mind, he's an eight, always was and always will be.

And since it's reasonable for anyone to aim high, as an eight, he could realistically stretch for one place above. Somebody who's a nine.

Trudy is undoubtedly a nine, if not a ten.

CHAPTER TWO

Trudy Andrews was an absolute stunner. She had long, wavy, thick blond tresses that tumbled halfway down her back. She rarely wore much make up, yet her skin was radiant and flawless. Her figure would grace any catwalk, and her face belonged on the cover of *Vogue*.

She had a trusting personality which unfortunately led to her marrying her childhood sweetheart. The relationship she fully expected to last until death parted them had not limped past four years.

Reality had bitten hard. The endless possibilities of youth faded fast when Trudy became a single mother. Nowadays her self-confidence was close to nonexistent

For years now she'd avoided men, devoted all her energies to her children. In those quiet moments, she told herself she led a fulfilled life. It was bullshit. Trudy was lonely. She was ready to get back in the game, she just needed a push.

One evening she was sitting in her local wine bar with her best friend Lucy Daniels.

The girls bore striking similarities in that both were

gorgeous with kind hearts; it was in their private lives that differences abounded.

Lucy possessed an abundance of confidence. She had played the field, gone on many dates before settling down with an architect who loved, respected and provided for her. The marriage was solid.

Trudy glanced up as a good-looking stranger walked in.

Lucy smirked.

"What are you smirkin' about?" Trudy demanded to know. "I saw that."

"Huh," Trudy replied, feigning ignorance. "Saw what?"

Lucy smirked again. They had been friends since they were five years old; she knew Trudy inside out. There was no need for words.

Trudy sighed. She was fooling no one and certainly not the girl who knew her better than anyone.

"Who'd want me with two kids in tow?" she asked.

"You're beautiful," Lucy insisted. "You could have any man in this room."

Trudy glanced again at the stranger.

"It would be nice to meet someone who's not a complete asshole," she admitted.

"Yeah," Lucy agreed. "He's definitely out there."

"A man worthy of love?" Trudy elaborated.

"You deserve someone special."

"You think such a creature exists?" Trudy asked doubtfully.

"Of course!" Lucy opined, optimism practically bursting from every pore. She believed it, why wouldn't she? She was living it.

Trudy considered the prospect. It seemed unlikely to her.

"They don't make men like your Seamus anymore," she decided.

"I disagree!" her friend said. "You just need to lower your expectations."

They both giggled.

CHAPTER THREE

The following weekend, fate threw Justin and Trudy together. It happened in Camden Town at a fundraiser for Syrian refugees.

Trudy was there because she religiously attended such events, cared deeply for those less fortunate than herself and wanted to make a difference.

Justin was there because it was close to his house and he was on the hunt for a new girlfriend.

He hadn't been there long before his eye fell on her. It was inevitable they would. She was the best-looking girl in the room by far.

'This is it,' he told himself, mistakenly thinking that what he felt looking at her could only be described as love. He moved closer to this vision in a red dress.

"People are living on the pavements of Hackney," he heard her say. "It's disgusting what they have to endure in one of the wealthiest countries in the World."

'Look at that passion.' Justin was spellbound. 'The way her nostrils flare when she emphasises a point. The way she flicks that shiny ponytail.'

She was fascinating. She was stunning. He moved closer still. He got so close that Trudy broke off her monologue and turned to look at the interloper.

Their eyes met.

He grinned like a naughty schoolboy.

'He's full of confidence,' Trudy thought. 'Maybe a bit too full.'

Justin ignored the people crowded around her.

"Hi, I'm Justin," he said.

"Trudy," she replied and allowed her hand to be shaken.

He bought her a drink and casually steered her away from the group she was with. He asked her about herself. He made an excellent job of pretending to be interested. And even though she didn't reveal much of a personal nature, she pontificated in great detail on what should be done to solve the plight of the homeless.

'I love her sexy voice,' he decided.

Justin had very little to add to the conversation that wouldn't show immediately he didn't have a clue what he was talking about, yet he desperately wanted to impress her. So when the collection tin came round, he donated handsomely, hoping she'd notice.

"Gosh, a hundred quid! That'll really help." Trudy smiled at him.

His little scheme was working.

"Well, you know, I think it's important we do what we can," he lied.

He added a shrug and a half-smile that was supposed to convey a deep sympathy for his fellow human beings.

"You know what I mean?" He said it as though injustice to his fellow man, unfairness to those less fortunate, hurt him deeply.

"I do," she agreed, nodding.

Justin was sure that nod really said, "Where have you been all my life?"

They had a few more drinks, and he listened attentively. When expected to speak, he settled for telling Trudy how interesting she was, how knowledgeable she was, and towards the evening's end, how sexy she was.

Before she left, Trudy gave him her number.

CHAPTER FOUR

A few nights later she was back with Lucy in the wine bar. They discussed kids, work, and all that was wrong in the world.

"How was that fundraiser the other night?" Lucy asked innocently.

Trudy blushed.

"Oh my God!" All innocence was instantly wiped from Lucy's demeanour. This was serious. "You met someone, didn't you?" she accused. "What's he like?" she demanded to know.

Trudy sucked her lip and wiggled her nose, clearly searching for the right words with which to answer the avalanche of questions.

"Is he cute?" her friend couldn't wait.

Trudy raised an eyebrow as though considering. She smiled and blushed a little. "So-so," she said.

"Did he try and bum any money off you?"

Trudy shook her head vehemently.

"No." She clearly objected to the slur on his character.

"Oh my God, you like him!"

They sipped their Prosecco, studied each other, both weighing up the situation.

Trudy not sure what she could say about him, what she even knew about him.

Whilst Lucy was wondering if she should offer her friend some condoms,

she leant forward. "I say shag him," she advised.

Trudy giggled. She pretended to be excited, but Lucy knew nervous laughter when she heard it.

"Did you give him your number?"

She nodded.

"Has he called yet?"

Trudy sipped her drink before answering.

"I'm meeting him on Saturday" she confessed, and Lucy shrieked, causing a few of the other patrons to look across at them.

Lucy leant over the little glass table and kissed her friend on both cheeks.

"I'm so proud of you," she declared. Beaming at her as though she were a child who'd just come first in the egg and spoon race.

"That doesn't mean I'm gonna do anything." Trudy tried to pour a little cold water on her friend's enthusiasm.

Lucy snorted. "Not this again?"

"What do you mean?"

"At least give him a chance this time," she advised darkly.

"What does that mean?" Trudy asked defensively.

Lucy sat back; she took a sip of wine. "You know what that means. It means, if you get the chance to do something nice, say yes!" Lucy lowered her voice, adding, "And if he wants to shag you, let him!"

Trudy snorted wine bubbles whilst failing to commit to anything.

CHAPTER FIVE

Saturday night came, and Justin had prepared well. He put on a new shirt and his best Hugo Boss suit. He made reservations at the ultra-trendy SkyView restaurant. He picked her up in a taxi, which went down extremely well. Trudy hated walking in heels.

As they rode through the streets of London Trudy studied him surreptitiously. She had to admit he scrubbed up nicely.

'Maybe I will shag him,' she thought as they were dropped right by the door.

'You can't shag him just because he saved you from getting a blister on your heel,' she realized, and uncertainty reclaimed its place in her decision-making process.

In the bar, they settled into plush window seats. Ambient music wafted over them, soft lighting added to the romance.

'She's gotta love this,' Justin concluded.

'It's nice to get somewhere new,' she thought.

The building tension was broken when the waiter came and took their order. Once he left, tension returned; Justin felt obliged to say something to break the spell.

"Have you been here before?" he asked.

Trudy shook her head. "Have you?"

"Once or twice," he admitted.

"I've been up there, though," she said and pointed through the window.

Across the river, the Shard soared into the night, high above all the other skyscrapers.

"Oh." There was a pause. "Why?" he asked.

"My little girl wanted to go."

"Oh," he said as they watched red and blue laser lights dance across the Shard's glass panels. London stretched out for miles beneath it. The view from their vantage point was undeniably romantic.

Trudy waited for him to say something.

'She's got a little girl,' he thought. Justin stole a glance at her. She looked incredible.

'Who cares,' he decided.

"You've got a little girl?"

"Yes, Megan, she's four."

"Oh, that's nice, I love kids."

He smiled to show he didn't mean anything weird by it.

'He won't want to talk about children.' Trudy stopped herself from extolling Megan's virtues.

He could feel butterflies floating around his stomach. A beautiful girl, a Saturday night and the city lights, He wouldn't have it any other way. This was what it was all about.

Add the anticipation, the build-up, the will we-won't we, into the mix, and you had the perfect recipe.

'The beginning is always the best bit about falling in love,' Justin thought.

He saw a different side of her reflected in the window. In her white cotton shawl over an elegant light blue dress, she truly was stunning from any angle.

"You look amazing," he told her.

She smiled at him,

"Thanks."

Their drinks arrived.

Trudy sipped her wine as he took a long slug of lager.

'At least he said amazing not nice,' she thought. She wasn't going to put out if he was boring.

'Don't be boring.'

Suddenly he swivelled around, and his eyes fixed on her. She was the centre of his attention. and it made her feel special.

"Do you believe in love at first sight?" he asked.

'Nothing boring about that for an opening gambit.' Should she be pleased?

"I dunno," she considered the question. "Yeah I suppose so," she decided.

"Me too," he shot back. They beamed at each other.

Trudy turned to the view.

'That was a nice thing to say,' she told herself. *'He's nice.'*

But there was a nagging voice at the back of her mind.

'What? Are you mad? What sort of a question is that to someone you barely know?'

For the briefest of moments, Trudy wondered if this was a huge mistake. But the view was nice, the wine was chilled, the babysitter had been paid.

Lucy's words sounded in her head: *'Give him a chance this time.'*

She vowed to wait and see how things played out, for Lucy's sake if nothing else.

A couple of hours later, Trudy was glad she'd persevered. After a few drinks, once he'd controlled his nerves, he turned out to be fun, attentive. He had stories that involved him getting into minor scrapes that, rather than leaving him bitter, had provided some amusing anecdotes. She had to admit he was good company; she wasn't to know the anecdotes were stolen from other people, normal people with interesting lives.

Justin knew how to seduce a girl, and Trudy was ripe for seduction.

He topped up her glass, he feigned interest in her stories, and he was on his best behaviour. It was the best date Trudy had been on for a long, long time.

They shared a taxi, which took Trudy home first.

"Do you want to come in?" she asked as it pulled into her street.

"Well, if you're sure. That would be great."

Trudy was planning to take him into the front room and relax on the sofa, but the room was a mess. She couldn't take him in there. She had asked her son to tidy up when his little sister went to bed. Possibly he'd been distracted; certainly, he'd forgotten to do so.

So they stayed in the kitchen, perched on stools on opposite sides of the breakfast bar, and the romantic factor dropped as the coffee levels in their mugs did the same.

With every creak of the house, Trudy thought her daughter would wake up. She couldn't relax.

Justin drained his drink as he realised the moment had passed.

"I best be off then," he announced, sliding back his stool and rising to his feet.

Trudy smiled.

"Thanks for a lovely evening. I really enjoyed it."

"Me too." He paused, wondering if she was going to come to him.

She stayed in her seat, so he zipped up his jacket.

"I'll call you," he said and headed down the passageway.

He heard the sound of a stool scraping across tiles, and he slowed down.

Trudy caught up with him.

"So I'll call you," he repeated.

"Ok," she said and leant across him to open the door.

Justin reached out and slid his hand behind the small of her back. He gently pushed, and she allowed herself to fall into a kiss.

But she knew the glass door meant they would be silhouetted for anyone who happened to be passing. However unlikely that may be late at night, she didn't feel comfortable, so she broke away and fumbled for the lock.

"Night," she said, casting her eyes bashfully downwards.

He pecked her on the cheek as he squeezed past her.

"Night, angel," he said, and he left.

Trudy closed the door and smiled all the way to the bathroom.

Justin did a little hoppity skip as he turned the corner and began searching for a black cab.

That was great. She's an absolute diamond.' In his mind the evening had gone extremely well.

'I'm in love,' he hastily decided.

The following Saturday he booked dinner and a show at Volupte, the hottest cabaret in town. Trudy wore a chiffon pearl-coloured dress that clung tightly to her curves, they laughed out loud at the compere, were thrilled by the dance acts, drank too much cheap wine, and couldn't keep their hands off each other in the taxi.

There was no time for coffee. A few minutes after getting in the front door, they were rolling round on the sofa interfering with each other's clothing. Very quickly, Justin was topless, and Trudy was down to her lacy underwear. The breathing was becoming faster, more frantic.

Then Megan awoke and started crying.

She stopped, so he stopped.

"You better go," she said, pulling her dress on over her head.

The way she wiggled into it drove him crazy.

'What?' he wanted to scream. *'Stop now?'*

But how could he? Megan's crying was growing in volume, clearly a signal that the party was over.

It was time to leave, and there was nothing that could be done about it.

"You can let yourself out, can't you?" She was already halfway up the stairs.

"Sure."

He did no little dances on the way home that night. If anything, he felt a bit frustrated.

'You'll be ok,' he consoled himself.

The weekend after that, Trudy arranged for her mother to have the children for the whole night.

She wasn't totally convinced there was a future with Justin; she didn't really know him well enough. But she liked him enough to get laid, she knew that much. Besides, it had been a while, she was horny, and Christmas was just around the corner. She didn't want to be alone again this year.

If Trudy ignored the nagging doubt in the back of her mind, it was fairly easy for her to pretend that things were looking up.

CHAPTER SIX

Justin, on the other hand, was experiencing no doubts whatsoever. Trudy was special, she was "the one," he was absolutely certain of it.

And with such knowledge, he was impatient to get on with it. To start looking at houses, arrange a joint bank account, or even meet her kids. Hell, he was ready to adopt them.

He definitely would when they got married.

He hadn't mentioned any of this to Trudy. It was probably too soon to get into details, he decided. But he let her know that he loved children, couldn't wait to meet hers.

"Everybody tells me I'm really good with kids," he lied to her, not for the first time.

Trudy believed him. She had no reason not to. She just wasn't sure inflicting her offspring on him would help their relationship necessarily. She felt they should probably get to know each other a little better first. But Justin was persuasive, and it was all new and exciting. She allowed herself to be talked round.

So on the night before Christmas Eve, they arranged to meet in the centre of town.

They would take in the Regent Street lights, pick up some last-minute bargains, and perhaps treat themselves to a burger. Justin had seen the ads; he knew kids liked going to McDonald's.

Trudy had to agree that in theory; it was a good plan, apart from McDonald's. She soon put paid to that idea, she wouldn't be seen dead in there, neither would her children. Well, Philip perhaps but certainly not Megan.

She had to agree with his basic sentiment though.

"Everyone's in a good mood at Christmas. It's a great time for us to meet each other."

'It might bring Philip out of his shell,' she thought. *'And I could put Megan's hyperactivity down to excitement. Pretend she isn't always like that.'*

Justin stood at the top of the steps of Oxford Circus tube station. It was extremely crowded. People kept jostling him. He didn't like it. He wasn't used to hanging around waiting. He spent very little time at the mercy of others.

He glanced at his watch.

'She's late.' If it had been anyone but Trudy, he would have left after five minutes. Somehow, mustering every drop of patience he possessed, he managed to hang in there for what seemed an age until finally he saw her. She was nine minutes late.

'Let it go,' Justin told himself. *'Best behaviour,'* he reminded himself.

"Philip couldn't make it," she announced as she approached.

Justin nodded and kissed her on the cheek.

"Well, at least you're here," he said.

He looked down at the child who had bothered to come.

"This is Megan."

The little girl was buried deep within a hooded parka.

"Hello, Megan." He smiled.

She stared back at him.

He held out his hand to shake. She continued to stare, her hands firmly in her pockets.

"Say 'hello' to Justin," said her mother.

The child half nodded.

"Take my hand," said Trudy and Megan did so.

As they wandered towards Regent Street, Justin tried to strike up conversation, but it was too busy for him to walk alongside them. They couldn't hear each other speak. How was he meant to get the child on side?

At the next big shop, he tugged at Trudy's sleeve, forcing her to stop. He pointed out a giant unicorn in the window.

"Look," he tried to inject amazement into the word

"Lame," Megan replied, tugging at her mother to continue walking.

Justin was surprised. He thought the little girl would be even more impressed by a giant unicorn than he was.

'Obviously not her thing. I'll try something else.'

He stopped again before a huge window with fairy lights all around the edges. The lights framed a display that consisted of hundreds of dolls piled high on each other. It truly was rather impressive.

'Little girls love dolls, everyone knows that,' he thought. *'She's gonna like this one.'*

"Look, Megan."

"Lame," she commented, barely giving the display a glance.

'She hates me,' Justin concluded. *'She knows I'm sleeping with her mum and she hates me because of it.'*

"What do you like?" he asked.

"What?" the child snapped.

"Nothin'" He felt the need to back off. he was wary of starting a conversation. She was making him nervous.

"Everything alright?" Trudy asked.

"Yes, Mummy." Megan smiled sweetly.

"I think she hates me," Justin told her quietly.

She snorted, which somehow suggested he was being ridiculous.

"Just be nice," she whispered.

He looked down at Megan. The child was staring at him, arms folded across her little chest, a stern look in her eye.

He smiled nervously, wondered what to say that could be classed as nice.

"What you staring at?" the kid demanded.

He forced laugher, but it came out more like a Bond villain than a Christmas shopper.

"You're weird," the little girl informed him.

He chose to ignore her. He needed a distraction.

"Look," he pointed.

"Now what?" Megan wanted to know. Her tone implied she was rapidly running out of patience with Mummy's new friend.

"Hamley's!"

"Never heard of it," said the child.

"Come on." he tried to grab her hand, but she was having none of it.

"Come on," he addressed Trudy.

She took Megan's hand, and they crossed the road.

Justin had formulated a plan. He decided it would be easiest to just buy her friendship.

He wondered how much he should spend.

He was still wondering as he crossed the road, Trudy and Megan momentarily forgotten. He took a risk with the traffic Trudy wasn't willing to emulate.

He waited for them on the other side of the street in the cold whilst seemingly invisible to the hordes. People kept jostling him again. He didn't like it, but he forced his smile to stay in place, managed to keep the impatience off his face. Once they were in the mecca of Christmas toys and Megan realised she had free reign, the atmosphere changed completely and everyone relaxed.

When he loaded them into a taxi an hour later, Megan was brimming over with the joy of Christmas. On the pavement outside Hamley's, despite being laden down with bags, she insisted on a big hug from Justin. He willingly obliged as Trudy looked on, smiling. He hadn't felt this Christmassy for years, if ever. It had been worth giving up an afternoon on the Xbox after all.

As far as he was concerned, the trip had been a complete success.

Trudy, on the other hand, was less sure.

She didn't believe children should get stuff just by pointing and saying, "That, I want that!" If she had known Justin was going to do such a thing, she would never have come.

Once he'd opened his big mouth, there was very little she could do. She tried to console herself that it was Christmas and all children deserved to be spoilt at this time of year.

And she had to admit it was wonderful to see her daughter so full of excitement but still...

Maybe things were moving too fast. She needed time to think straight.

She waited until the last minute, until they were parting ways.

"I have to go to my sister's after all," she told him through the taxi window.

She had warned him she might be unavailable over the festive break.

"Oh, I'll miss you," he said, surprised that he said it and even more surprised that it was true.

She smiled reassuringly. "Same here," she replied.

"I'll see you when you get back?" he asked.

She nodded as the cab pulled away.

CHAPTER SEVEN

J ustin had always found politics a bit of a downer.

It just didn't matter to him because, although he wouldn't consider himself rich, he was certainly comfortable. His grandfather had invented a widget that was copyrighted and is used on every single diving mask in the world. Justin didn't need to work. He was supposed to put in the hours at the office, but he rarely bothered.

The staff had it all under control. They didn't need him hanging around.

If ever his bank balance needed extra topping up, he simply asked his parents. They knew he would never repay a penny, but he was their only son. All parties concerned went through a charade purely to avoid potential embarrassment.

"I need some money to take a girl out, Dad. I'll pay you back next week."

"Here, son, take her somewhere nice."

"I need new front tyres for my car, Dad. I'll repay you at the end of the month."

"No problem, replace all four while you're there."

"I need a deposit for a bigger house, Dad. I'll return it when I get a lodger."

"No problem, how much do you need?"

Therefore it was difficult for him to relate to hardship. He did know people who took politics seriously. But they were friendships based on dope-smoking rather than political accord.

He once described himself as right-wing, but when asked what he meant by that, he had no answer beyond "because my dad is." The ensuing laughter stopped him from claiming to be anything publicly ever again.

When asked if he was against fire service cuts, he knew saying, "I don't really care. I'll be fine, my place has the latest detector and sprinkler systems," wasn't going to win him any popularity contest, so he took the easy option.

"Of course I'm against the cuts," he'd say.

If he gave World Affairs any thought at all, it was only ever in terms of how things affected him personally.

Selfishness was an unpopular position amongst dope-smoking lefties though, so when politics reared its ugly head, he rolled another joint, nodded and smiled, but he was miles away, in his happy place, not listening to a single word.

For Trudy, politics meant everything. The game was rigged, and she would not rest until the whole world realised.

She prided herself on keeping up to date on the latest developments, the trends and the intricate nuances of Westminster.

She attended as many meetings, rallies and speeches as she possibly could. Soaked it all up willingly. Local issue or global, it made no difference; to her, it was all part of a bigger picture. A right-wing global conspiracy where all roads led to the same handful of suspects every time.

There was no way Justin was going to admit his vaguely conservative views to Trudy.

Instead, he pretended to be thrilled when she invited him to accompany her to some tucked away community hall in Islington or Bethnal Green.

On one occasion he topped up his oyster card specifically to join her in a protest at the Ecuadorean Embassy. A week later they were side by side on a candlelit vigil in Brixton. He pretended to care; the truth was such outings often culminated in him getting laid.

At first, he'd tried to show an interest.

But as the weeks passed, he found he was usually mentally undressing her when he was supposed to be listening.

This became his coping mechanism every time she went off on an impassioned speech. Her politics could interfere with his enjoyment.

Today had been turned upside down, for example, because she had seen a homeless man being arrested.

Justin was getting the whole account, blow by blow. He was finding it hard to keep up because her blouse was unbuttoned one further down than usual.

"Don't you think?" he heard her say.

He was expected to have an opinion.

What to say, though? He hadn't been listening and besides knew nothing about hostels or even hunger really. Sympathy had always been a problematic emotion for him to project.

Perhaps she read as much in his demeanour.

"I'm talkin' too much, ain't I?" She delivered it as a question more than a statement.

"Nooo." He squeezed her hand and smiled. "Don't be silly."

She believed him. Why wouldn't she? She picked up her tale where she'd left off.

"So, the hostel was closed by the time we got him there..."

Justin tuned her out again.

'We've got nothing in common,' he thought. 'She's so hot, though.'

"Don't you think?" her voice broke through again.

He nodded seriously. Attempting to portray deep understanding.

"If only there were more people like you," he said.

She smiled and twitched her nose. "Aw, thanks, babe."

Justin smiled. 'Teething problems' he told himself. 'That's all. Once we're married, she'll forget about politics.'

His thoughts drifted, 'I could always trade her for one who prefers on-line shopping.' He nipped that thought in the bud. 'No, it's Trudy you love, nobody else.'

'She's so hot,' he reminded himself, because that trumped everything. Chased away all doubt. He knew he was shallow, but he was fine with it.

She was still talking, only now the frustration in her tone was growing more evident.

"Switch CNN on, babe," she asked, and Justin smiled and reached for the remote control.

"Sure, babe."

The way she devoured news made things worse, in his opinion.

'It's not like she can help everybody,' he reasoned, meaning, 'so why bother trying to help anyone?'

It genuinely mystified him the way she seemed able to make anything political, anything at all.

Privately Justin was rather pleased that he had identified this potential pitfall within their relationship. In his opinion, it wasn't insurmountable. He had already decided on a strategy; if he never disagreed, there was no argument to be had.

When she told him about some poor soul suffering terribly, he refrained from pointing out that he was fine with the suffering of distant strangers.

When she read a passage to him about political prisoners being tortured, he shook his head wistfully whilst thinking, 'I *know torture is painful. It's also painful to think about, so shut the fuck up.'*

He became skilled at checking her body surreptitiously as she vented. She was so beautiful, this was always guaranteed to offer him a certain amount of gratification.

"Trump's been President for three years now," she was saying.

She looked across in time to catch him nodding seriously. She wasn't to know he'd held the nod back until he knew she would see it. When she looked down to her screen, he secretly admired the erotic flash of skin visible between her top and her jeans.

"His attitude to climate change will be the death of us all," she was saying. "I can't believe he put extra tariffs on renewables, can you?"

"I know." Justin looked terribly upset.

"Renewables are where it's at," she sounded a bit angry now. That was good; angry sex was wicked.

"We'll be lucky if the planet has twenty good years left." She shook her head, and her eyes sparkled with frustration.

"I know," he agreed. "Bastards!"

"Where do you think renewables show most promise?" she asked.

He put on his serious face. He knew this one.

"We need more solar panels," he answered solemnly.

"Exactly," she agreed, "one's with a longer battery life. And I'll tell you where they should put them." and she was off.

She spoke with such confidence, such passion; her little cotton slip lifted and fell so tantalisingly, she was the complete package. It was a pleasure to behold. He could listen all night. Not fully listen, obviously, but be there in body if not in spirit.

'It ain't just cos I might get laid,' he tried to convince himself.

But his inner voice lacked the authority of Trudy's outer one.

He so desperately wanted to be in love, he vowed to try harder.

Her rhetoric slowed and finally stopped. It was his turn to say something.

"I've seen solar panels," he told her. "Miles and miles of them."

"Really?" she was willing to be impressed.

"Yeah, in the desert. In Morocco."

"Oh, the Chinese fields," she stated.

"No, in the Sahara, Moroccan."

She smiled gently, touched by his naivety.

"Chinese money," she explained.

"Oh," he replied. "They're cool, though."

The talk moved onto Morocco. She was interested that he'd been. So Justin's ego took over the conversation. By the time he finished talking, Trudy reasonably assumed he knew the whole country intimately.

He recalled wonderfully vibrant souks. He reminisced over the myriad of aromas. Painted romantic images of the food, the land, the people.

"I'd love to see it one day," Trudy sighed.

"We should go," he said immediately.

'What's more romantic than the call of the minarets as the sun goes down into the sea?' he thought.

Justin's memories of some years previous were rose-tinted by time.

He remembered vast sandy beaches, empty roads, wonderful food, easy natured people and excellent weather. Above all, he recalled cheap hash.

Time had conveniently erased the squalor, the beggars, the lack of basic amenities. This was partly because he enjoyed slumming it from time to time, taking little adventures to reinforce how lucky he was, before returning safely to Western decadence.

His thoughts strayed and a French girl he'd once taken abroad flitted across his mind. Africa had proven to be far more than she could handle.

He hadn't considered her for years. It was like a warning bell being switched on in his brain.

'Slumming it in Morocco is too much for nice European girls,' his voice of reason reminded him.

'It'll be different this time,' he insisted to himself.

The way he ignored the warning, dismissed it in a heartbeat, was magnificent. But whilst the blind optimism was certainly to be admired, it was incredibly naïve. Leaving no time to reconsider, banishing any second thoughts was a childishly hasty decision.

"You'd love it there!" he declared.

He should have stopped to weigh up the pros and cons, but who does that? Who, in the early days of a new relationship? He was thinking with his dick. Besides, he always acted in haste and wasn't likely to change any time soon.

CHAPTER EIGHT

It was a rainy Tuesday evening in North London. Trudy was sitting at her usual table in her local wine bar. She had a bottle and two glasses in front of her; she was patiently waiting for Lucy. She glanced towards the entrance, but her friend still hadn't arrived. All she saw were giant raindrops rolling down the glass door.

'Where is she?' she wondered. She was impatient for Lucy to turn up; she wanted to share her news. She'd spent the night at Justin's place last night, for the first time.

Finally, headlight beams flashed across the window. She looked out as an Uber pulled up in the deserted street. She watched the interior light come on and saw Lucy pay the driver. Then the car door opened, and with upturned collar, her friend scurried into the bar.

"Sorry," she mouthed as she approached the table.

Trudy rose to greet her. They air-kissed.

"Well?" Lucy asked before she'd even taken off her coat.

Trudy didn't reply. She glanced guiltily around the bar.

"How was it?" Lucy changed tack as she sat down.

"Well, he's got a nice place."

Lucy snorted and took a mouthful of wine.

She studied Trudy over her glass.

"I don't care about his place. Did you shag him?"

Trudy covered her mouth and looked around.

"Ssssh."

Lucy snorted again.

"Save it, sister," she said. "Nobody thinks you're still a virgin."

They smiled at each other as old friends do.

They both sipped their wine.

"Was he good?" Lucy asked.

"You're terrible."

"Are you going to see him again?"

Trudy took another mouthful of wine then told her about the suggested trip to Morocco.

There were questions, as she'd known there would be.

"So, let me get this straight," Lucy said finally, "he's offered to take you on holiday?"

She waited for Trudy to nod in affirmation.

"All of you, even Megan and Philip?"

She paused, and Trudy nodded again.

"He's a good shag?"

The nod came again accompanied by a knowing smile.

"And he's not overly political?"

Trudy frowned slightly at this final point of order. She slightly hesitated, but she nodded agreement.

Lucy gave her a stern look. "Whoa," she said. "Back up, sister. Let's be absolutely clear, non-political, that's a good thing."

"But all my friends are political," Trudy disagreed.

"I'm not."

"Yeah, but if we hadn't met at primary school, there's no way we'd be friends now," Trudy smirked as she spoke.

Lucy smiled easily. "I can't hold the fort alone. You need somebody else non-political in your life," she insisted.

Trudy sipped at the wine again. She had to admit he ticked

all the other boxes. Her friend had just gone through them in forensic detail. He passed all of them, all except one. It was now all she had left.

"There's just something about him, I don't know."

Lucy shook her head.

"You always think there's something sus about new people."

"I don't!" Trudy objected although they both knew she did.

"Just go!" Lucy pleaded. "What's the worst that can happen? You get a free trip to the sun?"

They both looked towards the lashing rain.

"Look at it out there," Lucy said unnecessarily. "I get the feeling he smokes too much dope," Trudy said.

She couldn't explain why she felt the need to sow doubt, especially with a free holiday up for grabs. The first free holiday she had ever been offered, by the way. She should be thrilled; she knew that. She just had a nagging feeling, a sense of unease, a cloud of impending doom.

"So what if he smokes a bit?" Lucy replied.

"I said 'too much.'"

Lucy shrugged; she wasn't really one for nuance.

"When are you seeing him again?"

"He's comin' over tomorrow."

"What are you going to say?" Lucy wanted to know.

"I'm gonna say this…" She took a large mouthful of wine for lubrication and recited as though she'd learnt the words by heart, "I've decided to take you up on your offer. It would be lovely to get away. This is a family trip though, so we'll be going as friends. We won't be sharing a bed."

Lucy snorted. "You can't say that!"

"Why not?" Trudy asked defensively.

"You seriously think he'll still wanna go?"

"Yeah."

"The poor guy. You'll be in your new bikini lying by the pool, and he's only allowed to look?"

"He'll be alright. He'll understand."

"Yeah, he'll understand the world is a cruel place."

"I'll shag him when we get back."

"Yeah, that'll do it."

They both laughed.

"I hope Megan likes him," Lucy opined.

The laughter stopped at the prospect of an unhappy Megan. Lucy saw concern flit across her friend's face.

"I'm sure she'll be fine," she insisted hurriedly, "sun, sea, er, sandcastles."

Trudy smiled, "Yeah," but her heart wasn't quite in it.

CHAPTER NINE

Their flight was leaving Heathrow early in the morning, so Justin had booked a hotel near the airport for the night before. He wanted to avoid any last-minute delays or stress-inducing situations, and, as an added bonus, thought it would be a treat for the little girl.

Justin was used to hotels; he liked them as a rule. He had never felt the need to stay in a family suite before, though. Nor had he ever spent the evening with a toddler.

Who knew they took so long to do everything, even the simplest of tasks? Or they could make so much mess in a bathroom?

And to cap it all, Megan refused to go to sleep because the ceiling was too high.

'The ceiling's too high? You're taking the piss,' he thought, whilst Trudy opted instead to take the more mature approach of assuring a child in unfamiliar surroundings that everything was perfectly safe and there were no such thing as ceiling monsters.

Only when she had been allowed to climb into the giant king-sized bed did she feel safe. Justin couldn't help wondering if the miraculous conversion was connected to her having the biggest bed. Maybe that had been her plan all along, he thought cynically.

'How devious are four-year-olds?' he wondered, *'and where am I supposed to sleep?'*

Justin hadn't slept in a single bed for many years. He tossed and turned until he was woken at first light because the kid was awake and wouldn't keep still or quiet.

First, she wanted to go to the bathroom, then she wanted some breakfast, then she wanted a story, and she constantly expected her mother's assistance with everything.

'That kid needs to toughen up,' Justin mused as he pretended to sleep.

He didn't factor in her tender age. He didn't really see it made much difference.

'Still,' he consoled himself, *'thing's will be better once we get there.'*

CHAPTER TEN

J ustin was asleep, dreaming about Trudy, yet a distant voice was making it hard for him to focus on the object of his desires. It sounded as though he was listening to a radio through a wall.

"Sir, sir, can you wake up please."

He frowned and pulled his arm further around his head.

"Sir, sir."

There it was again.

He opened his eyes. A stewardess was leaning over him. Her expression suggested she wanted to shake him none too gently.

"Could you wake up, please, sir? You're drooling on the lady next to you, and she doesn't like it."

"Sorry," he whispered to his fellow passenger.

A middle-aged woman glared back at him. She dabbed a tissue theatrically at her shoulder on what he presumed was his spittle.

Justin smiled sheepishly and wiped his mouth.

"Sorry," he repeated.

She said nothing, just glared.

He leant forward in his seat to look out the window but also so he couldn't see her glaring.

There was only blackness beyond the glass. He stared. His back was aching from falling asleep upright in a tiny seat. He could put up with it; it was better than facing his accuser.

He stayed hunched forward until the aching in the centre of his back eventually became too much to bear. He was probably forgiven by now, he reasoned.

He tried to wriggle back into a better position.

However, the wronged passenger alongside him had nothing better to do. She was on high alert and was determined not to share the armrest with such an unpleasant character. If possible, she planned to ruin the rest of the flight for him in any small way she could. For her, this was personal.

Justin gave up. It felt like he was bullying a pensioner; it didn't feel good.

Besides, they had been sitting together for two hours. During the first hour, he'd drunkenly tried to engage her in conversation. For most of the second, he'd used her as an unwilling pillow.

Now it was payback time.

'Seems fair,' he mused.

He took another glance towards the window. All he saw was the reflection of the interior of the plane. The woman next to him huffed under her breath.

'Alright luv, you're milkin' it now,' he wanted to say.

He looked across the aisle of the plane. There they were, his travelling companions.

Furthest from him, resting his head on the window, was Philip.

So far Philip had only spoken in monosyllabic grunts. He wore a chunk of black fringe permanently draped across his face, and the hood of his Megadeth sweatshirt was always up. It was difficult to be certain what lay hidden beneath.

He wore black nail varnish, and Justin was fairly certain, when he'd been forced to tip back his fringe for the customs agent, he'd caught a hint of eyeliner.

He didn't really know Philip yet. He assumed he was in possession of all his faculties.

Well, he had a passport. Justin supposed if he were a homicidal maniac his passport application would have been rejected.

And, he told himself, if somehow he had slipped through the net there, surely he'd have been stopped by one of the numerous security checks they had passed through at Heathrow.

'Still,' Justin thought, 'at least he don't ask for much.'

In the middle, cuddled up to her big brother, Megan was asleep.

She was so small she fitted the airline seat as though it were a bed. She looked angelic; Justin could easily see how he had been so badly mistaken about her.

'It was pretty unfair, though,' he couldn't help thinking.

Until yesterday they had only met the once, on the Christmas shopping trip. He'd foolishly assumed they had parted as friends.

The truth was as soon as she was denied permission to commandeer the remote control in their suite, she hated him and everything he stood for.

If he was honest with himself, it had shaken him rather deeply at how loud her screams could be.

Then this morning, echoing round an airport, she managed to scream even louder than she had the night before it seemed to Justin.

All because she left her dolly in the taxi.

Justin had needed to retire to the bar to gather his thoughts.

'I know she's just a kid,' he mused, nursing a whisky at eight am, 'but I told her enough times to look after her stuff. It's like she thinks you just say things for the hell of it!'

Still, she was sleeping now, and if a person didn't know better, they'd probably think she was a little angel.

Not the other passengers, of course. It was too late to fool them. They were under no illusions just how hysterical that cute little demon could get.

Justin's eye fell on the third passenger in the row.

In the seat just across the aisle from him sat the lovely Trudy. She was so close, he could have reached across and touched her. Not that he would dare. He risked another tut from the lady squashing him and leant forward a little further in order to steal a glance at Trudy's face. He quickly sat back again.

'That's not good,' he had to admit.

She wasn't actually crying. But she wasn't exactly not crying either.

Trudy had caught his movement from the corner of her eye. She turned to look at him.

She attempted a smile, but she was fooling nobody. Justin was spooked; he forced a return smile. What else could he do?

'What's up with her?' he wondered with good reason.

'She's fine,' he told himself. *'I'll do the English thing and pretend I didn't notice.'*

Then Trudy spoke. "Soon be there," she mumbled across the aisle.

He tried to think of something to say.

Something other than, "Have you been crying?" but he literally had nothing, couldn't think of a single thing that didn't contain the words "cry" or "crying."

She waited. Gave him a chance to come up with something, to start a conversation.

After a long, awkward pause, Trudy asked, "Can you see any lights yet?"

'Of course! I should have talked about the holiday, Idiot!' he admonished himself whilst twisting in his seat.

39

He took a quick peek through the window. "Not yet" he answered.

She sort of smiled again, but she had definitely looked better.

"Are you ok?" he felt obligated to ask. He hoped she would also play by the English rulebook and claim to be fine, regardless of what the evidence suggested.

"I'm fine," she replied and turned away.

'Good girl,' he thought and tried to leave it there, but reality had just been shown the cold light of day.

'She's on the verge of tears, for God's sake.' His mind wouldn't let it rest.

'She said she's fine,' he counter-argued.

The passenger hogging the armrest had followed the exchange closely. She was staring at him, burning a hole into the side of his head until she was impossible to ignore. He glanced at her for just long enough to see her shake her head.

'That relationship is doomed,' she hoped to convey. *'She's crying already, and you're not even off the plane!'*

Justin shook his head discreetly from side to side. He gave her a knowing smile.

'That's where you're wrong,' his smile said.

She huffed melodramatically and turned towards the window.

He glanced across at Trudy. Once again, she had her head buried in her hands. He daren't look. She might be in tears.

'Might be? Look at her shoulders, they're shaking! Go on, look!' his conscience demanded.

'She's alright,' he told himself.

He risked a quick glance, a double-check. She was still sitting with her head buried in her hands.

'She said she was fine,' he assured himself, choosing to ignore the evidence of his own eyes.

For distraction, he looked about the plane. Tried to convince himself that everything was indeed fine, although he had to concede things weren't exactly getting off to the ideal start.

Beside him, from the corner of his eye, he could sense the woman passenger was staring again. Daring him to meet her disapproving glare. He closed his eyes, denying her the contact.

'One to me I think,' he thought childishly.

CHAPTER ELEVEN

E verything was peaceful. Justin sat on a snowy white blanket with Trudy. She was dressed in a flowing cotton dress and looked absolutely beautiful. It was a gorgeous sunny day. They were eating strawberries and giggling together at a joke he couldn't quite recall.

She was stroking his arm as only lovers do. Now she was pulling at it. He frowned. The tugging became more insistent. He was forced to acknowledge it. His eyes opened, and the dream crashed and died.

"Sir, I have already spoken to you." The stewardess fixed him a withering stare. "You are drooling on fellow passengers again." She was making full use of her training, wearing the fixed grin that is practically a part of a stewardess's uniform and half whispering so as not to attract undue attention.

Justin had just woken up. He was never at his best first thing.

"What?" he asked, wiping his mouth.

"So rude," tutted the woman squashing him into the aisle.

"Sorry," he mumbled.

The looks they both gave him made it feel as though his apology had not been fully accepted.

He sat upright and vowed to stay awake. He daren't fall asleep again. There seemed to be consequences.

'What they gonna do, though?' he mused. 'They can't throw me off the plane.'

Even so, it felt like a point of principle now. Justin was determined to stay awake until they safely touched down in Marrakech.

His head lurched forward again, jolting him awake. This wasn't going to be easy.

Surreptitiously he pinched his thighs. He could feel the woman glaring at him. He looked across. She made sure he saw her disgusted gaze slip to his hands, then back to his face,

'I saw you,' her look accused. 'I saw you pinch yourself, you weirdo.'

Justin wanted to say "sorry" and throw her a smile. But he'd gotten so little sleep last night. He was too tired to mouth the word. His eyes started to droop. He pinched himself again.

The woman huffed rather too loudly. She'd seen him.

The tension in their little piece of aircraft was palpable.

In the row of seats across the aisle, a moan of displeasure rose in volume. The definitive sensation of tension spread through the cabin like wildfire. Incredibly quickly, the moan mutated into a piercing wail.

Very quickly, the hum of the engines, even the action movie at high volume were no match for the screaming.

Megan was awake. She had moved incredibly quickly from a wail of irritation into a series of screams that suggested she was in fear for her life.

Justin was unlikely to doze off now. He saw his least favourite stewardess heading towards them.

"Miss," he called, "could I get a coffee?"

He didn't want to ask for alcohol. He could only guess what judgement such a request would put on his head.

"Coffee is finished," she barked at him as she waltzed past.

'That's nice,' he thought. 'No 'sir' and no coffee.'

He tried to block the screams. They all did. Everyone on the plane, very few succeeded.

Trudy was attending to her daughter. Justin could see her mouth move, but the words were drowned out. However, it was having an effect. The screaming slowed, missed a beat and descended a little in volume. Now it could be described as loud intermittent sobbing.

Justin looked about the plane. Not one passenger was willing to catch his eye. They just sat and stared hard somewhere between their hands and the back of the seat in front. No doubt they all, each and every one, wished this journey were over.

As the noise seemed about to stop, some passengers began to glance around a little. They couldn't help it.

'She's going to stop,' the looks suggested.

'Things are going to be all right,' they dared to think.

"Is your little girl ok?" one brave individual asked Trudy. When Trudy looked up, another question was put to her, "Are you ok? You don't look ok!"

Trudy was about to answer.

Without warning rows of overhead lights appeared the length of the plane's interior. The aircraft bucked and wobbled unexpectedly.

Megan's screams filled the cabin.

There was a high pitched, grating click and the captain's voice came at them. He could just about be heard over the screaming child if one concentrated hard enough.

"Ladies and Gentlemen, please fasten your seatbelts. We are about to experience some turbulence."

The plane bucked and juddered. Megan screamed for all she was worth.

Justin smiled at the woman next to him.

"Could be a bumpy ride," he said.

She glared at him, huffed, shook her head and looked away.

MAKE OR BREAK IN MARRAKESH

Justin's eyes fell on Trudy. She was trying to wrap a blanket around Megan, who was screaming and kicking it violently off.

"Ladies and Gentlemen, please prepare for extreme turbulence," announced the captain.

As they dropped into free fall, Megan's screams filled the whole aircraft. Justin watched her kick her blanket to the ground.

'Please God, just make it stop,' he mentally repeated over and over as they plunged down through the sky.

Seemingly against all the odds, the pilot managed to regain control and the plane leveled out. It would have been worthy of a round of applause if the passengers weren't so badly shaken.

Upon landing, the subdued atmosphere of defeatism dissipated. A steely determination took its place amongst the plane's occupants.

Clearly, it was now every man, woman and child for themselves. You could feel it in the air.

Justin prepared to disembark.

He wanted to catch Trudy's eye, throw her a smile. Let her know he was ok; she didn't need to worry about him.

Trudy couldn't bear to look at Justin. Her face was apoplectic purple; she was right on the edge.

'Looks like Megan's upset her,' he surmised, incorrectly.

He glanced up and down the aisle. Privately mocked those rushing to retrieve their luggage.

'Amateurs, plebs, you should always shove everything in the hold.' He had no overhead bag, no paraphernalia, nothing. All he had to do was put on his jacket and wait for them to open the doors.

"Here take this?" Trudy snapped at him.

"What?"

"Stand up," she hissed.

It felt like a defeat, but he did as he was told. She loaded him up without catching his eye. Colouring books, empty drinks cartons, felt tip pens.

This wasn't what he had signed up for.

One of the pens had no lid on it. Red ink appeared on his hand and down the front of his t-shirt.

She hadn't given him a lot to carry. But it was all odd shapes. It was awkward.

Then without warning, Megan started kicking him.

"Move!" she snapped. "Move, I wanna move!"

She grabbed at Justin's knee and slid forward off her seat. She threw her little legs the short distance to the floor.

"Move!" she repeated.

Justin instinctively moved his legs away from being kicked.

"Don't let her go on," Trudy hissed.

Megan tried to force her way through the passengers.

"Wait," Justin hissed, grabbing her by the scruff of her neck.

Realising there was no way through the impatient mob, she allowed herself to be halted. She wasn't happy about it, though. She began to scream.

Justin flashed a random smile at the sea of scowling faces turning towards him.

She screamed all the way to the customs desk.

"Passports," demanded the uniformed officer.

Trudy glanced towards Justin. He released Megan's hand, and she immediately darted to her mother. They all watched as he patted his pocket. Juggled his armful of books and pens, patted his other pockets.

The customs man allowed him to go through the routine. When he started to go over the same pockets for a second time, however, he acted.

"Move aside," he ordered.

Not until every other passenger had passed through passport control were they acknowledged again. A girl in a light blue uniform approached.

She smiled nervously at Trudy. Glanced suspiciously at Megan and Philip. Then she addressed Justin.

"You 'ave your passaportes?" she asked.

"I had them on the plane," he replied.

She nodded as though she understood.

"Do you 'ave them now?" she rephrased her original question.

Justin patted himself down again.

"I had them on the plane," he repeated.

She smiled at him.

"Maybe you drop them?" she suggested.

It dawned on Justin that he had been holding them when Trudy had piled him up with Megan's stuff.

"Yes," he beamed. "They're on the plane. I remember."

"On the plane?" she repeated doubtfully.

"Yes," he insisted, "I remember."

The girl was shaking her head, sucking her lip and frowning.

"On the plane?" she repeated, sounding terribly unsure that such a scenario was likely.

"Yes," he insisted, "I remember."

She was still shaking her head, looking extremely doubtful but she picked up a phone and when it was answered jabbered something fast, in Arabic.

Her eyes never left Justin as she spoke. Clearly, he was the topic of conversation, and he had an awful feeling he wasn't coming out of it very well.

"It could happen to anyone," he half mumbled.

She gave him a half-smile. It was difficult to imagine a more sarcastic facial expression.

The call went on far longer than was probably necessary, but as Justin spoke nothing but English, he didn't have a clue. She could have been talking to her mother about the weather for all he knew.

Twenty minutes later, he was allowed back on board the aeroplane to look for the passports. He headed straight for the area where Trudy and the kids had been sitting. He stuck his arm so far down the side of the seat he nearly couldn't get it out again. He searched thoroughly but found nothing.

Then, looking bewildered and with far less enthusiasm, he searched around the area in which he'd been sitting. Again there was nothing. He stood up and scratched his head.

'Strange,' he thought.

He looked down the plane and saw the girl in the uniform watching him. He smiled at her. She gave him the sarcastic half-smile. She really had it down; he was mildly impressed.

It took another twenty minutes to satisfy himself they weren't there.

'That's really weird. I had them. I know I did.'

He shuffled towards the waiting girl.

"I can't find them," he said. "I had them. I know I did."

He looked defeated.

"Perhaps the cleaners take?" she suggested.

Justin stared at her gobsmacked. She was picking at her elegant fingernails.

'You couldn't have said that earlier?' he thought. *'You watched me for all that time. You couldn't have said something sooner?'*

"Yeah, maybe," he agreed, "We should ask."

She threw him the half-smile again. He wasn't impressed now; if anything, he found it annoying.

So, they filed in silence back to the main lounge. There was no need for words. Justin followed her, and she no doubt simply headed towards the screams they both knew could only be Megan.

Once reunited the little group traipsed noisily to the far end of the airport.

"No 'ere," answered the cleaner to their enquiry.

All the while, she was staring at Megan.

"Wha' wrong little girl?" she asked, crouching down.

In reply, Megan raised the volume.

"Maybe los' n foun'?" suggested the cleaner, hurrying back to her feet.

They began the long march back to the opposite end of the airport.

Justin was loaded up. He had his bag plus Trudy's, so she could carry her daughter. When they were about halfway, Trudy stopped.

"We'll wait here," she announced, plonking herself down on a plastic seat.

"Ok," Justin agreed.

He left the bags with her and continued.

He stood despondently at the lost and found desk as the attendant went off in search of his passport bag.

'She ain't going to find it,' he told himself. *'I wouldn't be surprised if she don't even come back.'*

Justin sneaked a glance down the huge empty building. He could see Trudy on her plastic chair.

'God, she's hot,' idly crossed his mind.

Megan had stopped bawling and was now whimpering into her mother's neck. Philip stood alongside them, his head bowed, his fringe hiding his face. His fingers racing across the screen of his phone.

'At least he don't complain,' thought Justin.

"Is this it?" The girl was back from her search.

Justin jumped at being addressed so unexpectedly.

She was holding out his passport bag.

He grinned broadly. All the traipsing the length and breadth of the airport had not been in vain after all. The staff he was convinced were completely useless had come up trumps in the end.

"Yes," he confirmed joyously. "That's it."

He could have kissed her.

She handed him a form to sign and passed him the cloth bag.

He opened the button on the flap and shuffled the passports up, revealing the top third of the hard red covers.

He started the triumphant march towards Trudy.

"Here they are," he declared, smiling. He knew the news would be sure to cheer them up.

"Huh," muttered Trudy.

"Here's what?" asked Megan.

"Our passports."

"Oh."

Philip didn't even look up.

Justin had more good news.

"Well, what about this then?" He pulled a folded sheet of paper from the little bag.

"It's a piece of paper," said Megan.

He was getting sarcasm from a toddler now.

"No," he forced a smile, "it's a bus transfer voucher."

Blank stares faced him.

"We're getting a bus?" Trudy asked.

"Yes, let's go find it," he replied, defeat heavy in his tone.

"There should be a sign," Trudy suggested.

"There!" Megan pointed at a row of overhead signs. One of which contained a picture of a bus.

The information was in English and Arabic.

"Buses to the left," the sign announced helpfully assisted by a giant yellow arrow.

"There we are," he said. "That way."

They trooped in silence to the big glass door, and Justin led them out into the warm night air. They turned left as the arrow instructed and almost immediately Justin saw little numbered shelters. He had to admit the signage system was faultless.

There may have been shelters, but there were no buses. No vehicles at all, in fact, nor people.

"Funny, you'd expect it to be busier," Justin observed.

He stopped and unfolded his sheet of paper.

"It should be at bay number eight." There was a definite hint of surprise in his voice.

They all stared at bay number eight. There was no bus. There were no buses in any of the bays.

"Maybe it's not here yet," Justin suggested.

Trudy gave him a look of disdain she didn't bother trying to conceal.

The moon was high. The night air was filled with the aroma of bougainvillea and the sound of cicadas. It was a world away from North London, idyllic even, if you ignored the fact they were stranded.

"What are we going to do now?" Philip wanted to know.

Their predicament was momentarily forgotten at the sheer surprise of him asking a question. They seemed like the first words he'd spoken all day.

"Are you all right dear?" asked his mother.

Megan had wandered slightly. She could see around the airport building from her new vantage point.

"Taxis!" she announced.

They rushed to join her and sure enough in a brightly lit, busy part of the airport were a row of gleaming white Mercedes cars with little yellow lights on top.

"What are those people wearing?" Megan wanted to know.

"They're hijabs," her mother replied.

"I want one," the child announced.

"Wait!" Trudy barked. "Hold my hand! Let's just get a cab," said Trudy.

Justin nodded.

He forced a smile and approached the taxi rank. Trudy followed a couple of steps behind. Megan dragged alongside her, sliding her feet across the tiles, slowing her mother down. Philip brought up the rear; he was looking at his phone.

As Justin neared the front of the queue, a car door flew open.

A beast of a man with a full head of thick, shiny, black hair jumped out. He smiled broadly,

"Inglish?" he asked.

"Yes," Justin replied.

The man produced a large square of white cotton and flicked imaginary dust off his bonnet in a practiced fashion. "You want to go to town?"

"Yes."

"80 Dirham," he said.

Justin nodded gratefully. "That's fine," he replied.

Their luggage was hefted into the boot whilst Trudy and her kids climbed into the back seat.

Justin sat alongside the driver. He watched him turn the key and rev the engine unnecessarily.

Where you wanna go?" the taxi driver asked as they raced away from the airport.

Justin produced his sheet of paper. He'd had mixed results with it so far, but he had no choice other than to persevere.

"Riad Rahba," he pronounced the words carefully. He fully expected the driver to tell him there was no such place and throw them out of his vehicle.

"Ahhhh, Riad Rahba." The man beamed wide as he beeped his horn at a moped. It had maneuvered into a tiny space inches from their front wheel.

He turned to Justin. "No problem," he said happily.

Justin smiled nervously; he'd prefer the man watched the road.

"There's no seatbelt," Megan stated loudly.

"We no 'ave," said the driver.

"They don't have seat belts," Megan repeated in wonder. Such a prospect had never occurred to her.

"Mummy, they don't have seatbelts."

Trudy draped an arm around her child.

"I'll be your seatbelt," she said.

Megan smiled.

The traffic was heavy, and Justin felt they were too close to the car in front.

"Is it far?" he asked.

"Riad Rahba is no far," replied the driver happily.

He turned to face Justin alongside him.

"Welcome to Morocco."

"Thanks," said Justin staring nervously ahead, trying to get him to watch the road without criticizing his driving.

They were racing along. Part of four lanes of traffic all heading vaguely east. There was an awful lot of horn blowing. The vehicles came in all shapes and sizes. A kid on roller-skates flitted across the lanes with daring skill. A giant lorry attempted to turn left. Pandemonium reigned.

It was bizarre that their driver seemed to think watching where he was going unnecessary.

He turned around to address the passengers on his back seat.

"Welcome to Marrakech." He hadn't stopped beaming yet.

"Thanks," replied Trudy.

"Mummy, you're hurting me," said Megan.

She hadn't realised she was clutching her daughter's arm quite so tightly.

"Sorry," she mumbled, releasing her grip.

Trudy was used to the traffic of London, but she had never seen anything like this. She tried not to look.

"Stop staring at me, Mummy." Megan frowned.

"Sorry," she mumbled again.

After a while, the taxi began to slow. Then the sheer volume of traffic meant they were soon reduced to a crawl. Justin spotted some camels lounging beneath palm trees.

"Look!" he said enthusiastically. "Camels."

Megan poked her head out from behind Trudy's arm at this information. But she was so slow facing in the right direction, even at crawling speed, the camels were somewhere in the distance by the time she got a bearing.

"I wanna see the camels," she whined.

"Look," Justin tried a distraction technique.

He pointed skywards, and this time she followed his finger with her eyes. It looked like stars dropping to the ground. Neon blue ones leaving a trail as they fell. Toy lights being catapulted high into the night sky. All the way up and all the way down again.

Megan was four. She couldn't help but be impressed.

"What are they?" she asked in amazement.

"They look like shooting stars," he told her.

"What are shooting stars?"

Justin couldn't be bothered to explain.

"I think they're toys," he said instead.

"Can I have one?" came the obvious response.

"We'll see," interrupted Trudy.

The neon toys emanated from a crowd in a giant square that the taxi crept towards. Thousands of people were milling about. Men, women and children of all descriptions, from all corners of the globe.

There were rows of brightly painted wagons, displaying aromatic foods and ice-cold drinks. There were African drummers, Spanish dancers, and tourists from all points of the globe.

Snake charmers offered photographs with cobras and pythons. Old women offered henna tattoos.

Everything was negotiable. Nothing seemed permanent. It was the epitome of organised chaos.

Suddenly the taxi stopped. The driver jumped out with impressive speed, and in an instant, he retrieved their luggage from the boot and piled it on the pavement.

Crowds encroached towards them. Trudy was first out. She was worried the bags were going to be stolen. The bewildered little group climbed from the car behind her. Megan rushed to her mother and clung to her legs. She looked ready to switch on her special panic alarm, it seemed to Justin.

The driver pushed his way through a gaggle of children towards Justin. He thrust out his hand and smiled.

"Eighty dirham," he said.

Justin paid him the agreed amount, and the driver climbed back behind his wheel, turned his key and began to rev the engine. The crowd moved away from the bonnet of his car.

Trudy frantically poked her head through his window to prevent him leaving.

"The hotel?" she asked.

She couldn't see any hotels.

"Da da."

He pointed vaguely to the right. A narrow street was running off the main square.

"Da," he grinned proudly, "Riad Rahba."

As she stood up to look, he drove away, clearing the crowd before him. The mob of people surged forward again like a wave as he passed. Children with their hands out crowded around Justin in particular, repeating a word unknown to the English visitors. Megan began to wail.

Suddenly one loud voice rose above all others.

"Get back!" someone screamed in English in a tone surprisingly high for a fully-grown man.

The stranger approached, smiling. He repeated his order. Justin reached to cover his ears. This guy even drowned out Megan, no mean feat.

"Get back," his high tone cut through the din.

He gestured at Justin with double thumbs up and a beaming grin that only seemed to emphasise his lack of incisors.

"Hey? English, I speak English. How you like that?" he asked.

Justin smiled and returned the thumbs up with both hands.

The man's grin vanished to be replaced by a grimace of a far more intimidating nature. He raced through the crowd of mainly children, swishing his arms about. He didn't try overly hard to make contact, and the street urchins took no great offence. They easily kept beyond his reach. But he was making a difference. The crowd thinned. He came to a halt alongside Trudy.

"I speak English," he stated again.

He swivelled his head from side to side. Taking in the newcomers with his beaming smile and his uneven teeth.

"We are looking for Riad Rahba?" Trudy ventured.

"I will take you," he exclaimed almost before the words were out of her mouth.

"Are you sure?" she replied doubtfully.

"Of course, pretty lady. Salim will take you." He brought his heels together in a military fashion.

"You're Salim?" Justin asked.

"I am, and you are?"

"Justin," he said. He moved closer to shake Salim's hand. "Pleased to meet you, Salim," he added, genuinely meaning it.

"This is Trudy," he gestured. Salim glanced at her.

"Hello," he said.

"Hello," she replied.

"This is Philip," Justin announced.

Philip seemed thrilled to have Salim's help. He must have been because he actually acknowledged the man.

"Huh," he grunted.

Salim touched his forehead and mumbled something in Arabic.

"And this is Megan," Justin said.

They all watched as the big man lowered himself to his knees and gently made Megan's tiny hand disappear inside his giant paw.

"It is my honour to make your acquaintance," he stated solemnly.

Megan shivered with delight and allowed her hand to be politely shaken.

'*She's spellbound,*' Justin realised. '*Mind you, I almost love him myself right now.*'

Justin held out his sheet of paper.

"Do you know where this place is?" he pointed at the name.

Salim wagged his finger.

"We don't need map. Riad Rahba, I know it, everyone knows it. It is this way, come. I will give you the guided tour."

He grabbed the handle of the large suitcase and began to wheel it. The few remaining urchins parted before him. He stopped and turned.

"This way," he repeated.

Trudy gave Justin a look.

'*Do you think it's safe?*' the look asked.

Justin grinned at her. He completely missed the implied question.

"He seems nice, don't ya think?"

She smiled. It wasn't a convincing smile, but she was tired and hungry.

Her children hadn't moved. They were waiting to see how things panned out. Whether their mother was actually going to make them follow a complete stranger in a foreign land. After all the lectures she'd given them, she was intending to trust him with not only their suitcase but with their very lives.

"Should we go with him?" Trudy ventured.

"It'll be fine," said Justin.

And she could see that she didn't really have a lot of choice.

"Megan, take my hand," she said.

Megan, surprisingly, did as she was told immediately.

Trudy raised an astonished eyebrow towards Justin.

"Well," she said, "fancy that."

'*We're sharing a moment,*' Justin thought happily.

Once Trudy had hold of her daughter, she did something

Justin would never forget. Without any preamble or fanfare, she slipped her lovely, soft, manicured left hand smoothly into Justin's right and with a

"Come on, Philip, don't get lost," she had put her trust in Justin.

Gratefully, he looked at her and smiled, but she wasn't ready to go that far. It was too soon after the airport fiasco to acknowledge the massive step she had just taken.

His heart was beating like a drum; his pulse was racing like an express train. A longing for her tore through every fibre of his being.

'This is gonna be fantastic,' he told himself.

CHAPTER TWELVE

S alim bumped their suitcase along uneven paving slabs, then bounced it across cobbles before hitting a dirt track, where it was mostly being dragged.

Trudy watched horrified at the rough treatment of her precious possessions. Justin didn't notice.

Salim set a healthy pace. There was no time for taking in the surroundings. Hell, there was no time to even look at the person next to you, it seemed.

Justin didn't care. He squeezed her hand.

'I knew she loved me,' he felt giddy with joy. 'This is the real thing,' he told himself happily.

They followed Salim through one narrow street after another. They could easily have been going around in circles. He could have been lulling them into a false sense of security before he took them to an isolated spot where they would be robbed and murdered and their bodies found in the cold light of day.

The thought crossed Justin's mind, but he wisely decided not to say anything.

They were completely lost. They needed Salim now. There was no way Justin could find his way to the Riad.

He made an effort to ooze nonchalance. He pretended they were in a movie.

They passed ochre-coloured, faded, patchy plaster on buildings. Exotic stalls piled high with shiny trinkets. Giant clay pots filled with aromatic spices and people in wonderfully quaint traditional outfits.

'I love it here,' Justin decided.

'I hate it here,' thought Trudy.

"It's like a movie set," he said.

Trudy glanced at him but refrained from replying.

"Aladdin," said Megan.

"Yes," agreed Justin.

Without warning, Salim stopped.

Theatrically he spun round and counted them off. Satisfied they were all still present and correct, he set off again. This time he led them across the crowds. He waddled like a mother duck. They kept close like helpless ducklings.

Justin felt Trudy grip his hand tighter; he resisted the urge to look at her. He was worried concern at their current predicament might show on his face and freak her out. He satisfied himself with a little squeeze back.

They followed Salim wondering how they had ended up here. In a strange land with a strange man leading the way.

This was nothing like North London.

Justin loved it.

'This is real,' he thought. *'I feel like I'm alive.'*

Beside him, Trudy too was deep in thought. *'He could be leading us into a trap to kill us all,'* she reasoned.

Trudy squeezed Justin's hand not realising she was giving him a sexual thrill. His whole body tingled at the prospect of what might be.

'I'm on an exotic trip holding hands with a beautiful girl. It don't get much better than this.'

Trudy convinced herself Salim was going to murder them all for a suitcase full of old clothes whilst Justin did nothing.

She glanced about her at the badly lit track.

'What a horrible place to die,' she thought.

Salim stopped again.

"I gave you the scenic route," he beamed proudly.

"Are we there yet?" asked Megan.

"It's a real adventure, innit?" Justin said.

Trudy kept her thoughts to herself.

She squeezed past Justin. She threw him a look as she did so.

'This is not an adventure,' her look suggested.

Justin stared after her, baffled.

'She's probably tired,' he decided.

"This is my best scenic route ever," said Megan.

'This is great,' Justin thought.

"Where are we going, Mummy?" Megan's voice broke through Justin's thoughts.

"To the hotel," Trudy replied. She sounded neither certain nor convincing. "Aren't we?" She turned to Justin for reassurance.

"That's right," Justin beamed at her. She looked away.

'If he grins at me one more time I'm gonna scream,' she thought.

'She seems tired,' he figured. *'Probably all the excitement.'*

"Are we there yet?" Megan wanted to know.

"Yes, my little English princess, we are there," Salim told her.

Trudy stared aghast as he rapped on a tatty old door.

"This is it?" said Megan.

"It sure is" Justin agreed.

A young boy of about Megan's age pulled the door open. He was dressed in a traditional white robe and greeted them as solemnly as an old man would.

Salim replied with a barrage of Arabic at the end of which the infant pulled the door wide open and ushered them all in.

The interior looked to be in slightly better condition than the door.

A small desk faced them. It held an old-fashioned landline telephone, a book for guests to sign, and an overflowing ashtray. Behind it was a large, padded armchair and on the wall behind that a portrait of the King.

Justin took all this in. Only when he looked again did he notice a wizened old woman sitting in the shadows to his left.

"Have they got wi-fi?" asked Philip quietly.

They all turned to look at him. Twice he had spoken now since they'd landed.

There was a brief pause before Justin answered. "I'll ask, shall I?"

Philip nodded. Justin waited with bated breath for some accompanying words, but there was to be no more. Perhaps he had used his quota for one day.

Justin faced the old woman. "We have a reservation," he said.

She stared back at him, her expression completely blank.

"Do you have wi-fi?" he asked.

She continued to stare.

Salim let fly a volley of words.

With an indignant sigh and a cloud of dust, the woman rose from the chair. She went behind the desk and flicked through the register.

"Tondidori?" she asked.

"Yes," Justin answered, "that's me."

There was another volley of Arabic from Salim. Quieter this time, less staccato, accompanied by his toothless grin.

The old woman replied with a few words.

"Her grandson will show you to your rooms," Salim translated.

They began to gather their belongings and prepared to be led to their rooms.

"So I shall go," Salim said.

"Thank you," Trudy told him.

"Yeah," he seemed dissatisfied.

Justin stepped forward and pressed a few notes into the man's hand. "Thanks for your help," he said.

Salim muttered something that was probably a blessing and reversed himself out of the little foyer.

When he had gone the designated child led them upwards until they came out onto a flat roof. White sheets were drying in the breeze. The boy ducked under them as he crossed the roof. They all did likewise.

He headed directly to a pair of doors where he waited for them to join him, and with an extravagant flourish, he opened both simultaneously. He stepped back as though half expecting his audience to applaud.

Trudy stuck her head through the first door. Her nose wrinkled and she backed out. In silence, she went to look at the alternative option. It was the same, exactly the same.

Twin metal beds, each covered with a sheet and a thin, old-fashioned, threadbare blanket. The fixtures and fittings consisted of a tiny chest of three drawers and a solitary hard-backed chair.

Trudy's face suggested she had expected something a touch more luxurious, although at this stage she would willingly settle for furniture that didn't look as though it had been on Earth longer than the old lady in the foyer.

The child said something to Justin.

"I dunno what you're saying."

"Yes. Yes," hissed the boy, nodding all the while,

"Mr. Tondidori," he said it like it was a question.

"Yes," Justin agreed

The boy slipped a pair of keys into Justin's hand. Bowed like an actor about to leave the stage, and with the briefest of glances towards Megan, he turned on his heel and flew across the tiles. He took the corner so fast Trudy covered her mouth and gasped. She was terrified he was going to slam into the solid staircase.

Megan giggled; despite her lack of years somehow she instinctively knew he'd performed that daring manoeuvre for her benefit.

The impressed little girl raced to look over the inner wall. The boy was halfway down looking up, waiting for her to appear. They smiled conspiratorially at each other. No adults caught the exchange. And that was all it took. From now on, they were firm friends.

Justin wasn't even looking their way.

"Wow," he said, staring out over the rooftops. "Look at this view!"

They were in the heart of the ancient medina. He was looking down on the old walled city in all its glory. It was noisy, busy, hot, and bursting with life.

"Look!" he pointed.

'They're gonna love this,' he thought.

They came slowly, but they came.

"Huh," said Philip seemingly unimpressed.

"It's high up," said Megan.

"Have you seen these rooms?" asked Trudy. She beckoned him to come and see.

"What's wrong with them?"

"When did you last see blankets like that?"

"I dunno, I think my gran had something similar."

"Exactly."

He looked at her, confused. "Er, yeah." He smiled. "Oh look, cool, we've got shutters."

There were shuttered windows that opened onto the terrace. Trudy shook her head in disbelief. She headed towards a door set into the far wall. A quick look confirmed it contained a musty old shower and 1970s style toilet. She didn't go inside.

Justin had gone out onto the terrace. Now he was poking his head in through the shuttered window.

"Hello," he joked as she moved away from the bathroom.

"Yeah." She smiled but didn't look particularly amused.

"Megan and I will take this one." She indicated the room on the left. "Ok?" she added as an afterthought.

Justin nodded. "Sure," he said. "We don't mind, do we, Philip?"

Philip shrugged.

There wasn't much to say. Now that he knew which was his room, Philip stepped through the allotted door and slumped down onto the nearest bed. He was fiddling with his phone before the dust had settled around him.

"Trying to get wi-fi, are ya?" Justin asked.

Philip glanced at him but declined to answer.

Justin threw his little bag on the vacant bed.

CHAPTER THIRTEEN

The next morning Justin was woken by a scream. He leapt from bed and rushed out onto the roof terrace just in time to see Megan scream again.

Justin took in the scene before him, and even though they were screams of excitement, he covered his face in horror.

She was running at full speed, her little arms outstretched like aeroplane wings. She banked to her right, her left, stole a glance at the young boy who'd shown them their rooms the night before.

Suddenly it made sense. It was still an accident waiting to happen, but at least it made sense.

A short distance ahead of Megan, fresh laundry had replaced the sheets of the night before. Water was dripping onto the shiny ceramic tiles.

For one so small, she was eating up the space. It was quite impressive, just a shame she was oblivious to the impending doom.

'*Oh shit*,' Justin thought just as Trudy appeared at his side.

Like him, she took in the scene at a glance, simultaneously

realised her daughter was in deep trouble and tantalisingly out of reach.

Trudy's hands rose to cover her mouth. She screamed something, the first part of which was "Slo—"

'Probably telling her to slow down.' Justin liked little guessing games with himself, even at the most inappropriate moments.

Side by side, they watched helplessly.

There was a tortoise at the far end of the patio. Its dark shape stuck out against the clean white tiles.

'Clean, wet tiles.' Justin glanced at the puddle between Megan and the tortoise.

She hit the puddle at top speed. She never really had a chance. She lost traction and went into a sideways skid. She adjusted her balance admirably, and for a brief moment, it seemed she was going to pull off the impossible manoeuvre.

She bent her knees, lowered her centre of gravity. Running on pure instinct, the kid did everything by the book.

It was a courageous effort yet futile. She slammed into the corner of a solid iron table. It forced her to an immediate halt, and the wails of pain began before she had fully dropped to the floor.

The Moroccan boy was first to her side.

'Where did he come from?' Justin wondered. *'Why didn't he fall over?'*

The boy jabbered away at her with such concern on his face that it truly threw them all, even Megan.

'She can't be that badly injured,' Justin assessed as he moved closer, *'or she'd still be screaming.'*

"Megan!" Trudy pushed Justin aside in her haste to the scene.

'Bit rude,' he thought.

She crouched to her daughter, expecting the worse, broken bones and trips to third-world hospitals.

Incredibly, the child seemed to be fine. Her new friend had everything under control.

Megan didn't understand his words. It didn't matter. She had the undivided attention of a stranger. This was a first for her.

She pointed to her knee.

He gently inspected it.

She pointed to her hand. He took it with great respect and examined it thoroughly.

Justin came up alongside Trudy.

"Aren't they cute?" he said.

She glanced at him and smiled. It was a nervous, uncertain little smile that Justin took as a green light.

He threw his arm across her shoulders and partly through shock, partly relief she didn't push him away.

They stood in silence, letting the scene before them play out.

Justin took a little perverse satisfaction from the close proximity. He half knew he was taking advantage of her, but it was nothing his conscience couldn't live with.

He watched Megan point at the tortoise. The boy rose and fetched it to her.

She was beaming now, the shock of slamming into the table seemingly replaced by the joy of having a new playmate. One who seemed satisfied to do her bidding.

She took the offered tortoise, which immediately withdrew its head.

The two children looked at each other before bursting into laughter. The incident with the table was already far behind them.

The muezzin began to wail, calling the faithful to prayer. Justin glanced across at Trudy.

'This is really exotic,' he thought. 'She's gotta love this.'

Trudy smiled back at him.

"Do you think she's ok?" she asked, nodding towards the daughter who seemed to have forgotten they were even there.

Justin nodded.

"Looks fine to me," he said.

'Looks like she was faking it,' he thought.

This was what he'd been waiting for. They were already embracing, their lips inches apart, Justin leant in for the kiss.

"Mummy look!"

Megan held the tortoise up to show her mother and the moment passed.

"It's lovely darling," Trudy replied,

"Can I keep him?"

"He lives here darlin'."

"Can I play with him?"

"Perhaps you can play with it once we have our rooms sorted."

"It's a him, Mummy, not an it!" She frowned.

"Sorry, he. Has he got a name?"

Megan turned and solemnly, very slowly, asked the boy in English.

He beamed. "Yas," he replied.

"He's called Yaya," she paraphrased.

"You play with him, I'll sort out our room."

All else was forgotten as the tortoise tentatively poked its head back out. Not sensing any immediate danger, its legs protruded and began thrashing back and forth.

"Look, Mummy!" she squealed excitedly. "He likes me!"

"That's lovely darling," Trudy said, already turning away. She walked towards the two rooms

"How's your room?" he asked.

"What?"

"You know, did you sleep all right?"

Trudy gave him a look that suggested he had taken leave of his senses.

Justin returned to his room.

"Want to have a look around?" he asked Philip.

The teenager looked up briefly, shook his head and looked back down at his screen.

"Mind if I do?"

Justin's question was greeted with a shrug.

It was then they heard Megan scream. "He bit me!" she wailed. "He bit me."

Justin went to see what had happened.

Trudy was ahead of him.

The Moroccan boy was ahead of them both. They watched as he inspected her hand once again. Clearly, there was no real harm done. Again she was pacified by his undivided attention. Trudy smiled at Justin as they watched.

They listened to the boy jabber gently away at her. They watched the children make a mockery of the language barrier.

"They understand each other perfectly," said Trudy.

As the muezzins wailed all around them, Justin casually slipped his hand into hers.

"Yeah," he agreed.

She pulled away.

"I'm going to unpack, have a shower. You ok to watch Megan?" she smiled. But he could tell by the way she had blurted out the words that he had flustered her.

Justin nodded. "Of course," he said.

He went and sat in the shade, adjusted the erection in his trousers. The rooftops of the old city crowded all around. Justin observed how compact the living conditions were. He listened to the call to prayer, revelled in the exoticness of it all.

Then he saw something move on the neighbouring roof. It was a cat. He watched it lying in the shade. And as his eyes adjusted to the light, he spotted another. He walked to the edge of the roof and scanned around him. There were cats everywhere.

'They've got their own cat world up here. They can cover the whole city without touching the ground,' he realised.

The more he looked, the more he spotted. Feline silhouettes lazing in the shade of broken chimney pots and a multitude of satellite dishes. Just chilling beneath the intensity of the African sun.

Justin could hear the bustle of the people below. His nostrils caught the unfamiliar scents of the bazaar and the souk, and he was overjoyed.

'*This is real living,*' he told himself, smirking without realising he was doing so.

He watched a battle-weary tomcat stretch on a ledge. It was clearly king of all it surveyed.

'*Lies there all day, no doubt,*' Justin mused.

"What you lookin' at?" Megan wanted to know as she appeared at his side.

Justin turned round and smiled at her. He nodded a greeting to the Moroccan boy who lurked over her shoulder.

"What's his name?" Justin asked.

"Malik," she stated matter-of-factly.

Justin shook his head in mild amusement,

'*How the hell does she know that?*' he wondered.

"What you doin'?" she asked again.

"I'm looking at cats," he told her.

"I like cats," she declared and climbed up on him.

Justin wasn't used to children. He had no idea that four-year-olds shouldn't be encouraged to climb on rooftops.

The boy Malik seemed to have a much better grasp of the situation. Silently he slipped to Trudy's room and tapped on the door.

When she appeared, he needed do no more than glance across to Megan.

Trudy shrieked.

"Get her down!"

She marched the short distance and grabbed Megan up in her arms.

"What are you doin'?" she demanded

"Just looking at cats, Mummy."

Justin was about to add something but the look Trudy threw his way made him think better of it.

"Don't let her climb up," she scolded him.

'Jeezus what's her problem?' he wondered.

With his feelings slightly hurt, he sauntered across to the room he shared with Philip. He popped his head around the door to see the teenager still sitting on his bed. Head bowed, fingers racing across his phone.

"What you doin'?" Justin asked.

Philip glanced up, looking as though he was about to speak. Justin waited with bated breath.

'Are we about to have a conversation?'

Philip looked as though he was about to speak, but at the last minute, he decided not to. He shook his head wistfully and returned to his game or text message or snapperchatter or whatever the kids did these days.

Justin also looked as though he was about to speak. However, he chose not to. He smiled pointlessly and went back out onto the roof terrace.

'I need to score,' he decided.

CHAPTER FOURTEEN

Coming back into the sun, the first thing he heard was Megan asking if cats ate tortoises.

"No, dear, they wouldn't be able to get through the shell."

He smiled at Trudy's patient reply.

"What do they eat?"

"They eat fish, dear, you know that."

"Oh yes, fish, I knew that."

"You're really good with her," he said, approaching them.

The look she gave him wasn't completely cold.

'She definitely likes me,' he thought.

"Can I just see if he wants it?"

Megan wasn't convinced that cats didn't eat tortoises.

Her mother shook her head, and the child sighed theatrically. Malik hung back, his look halfway between concern and adoration.

"I wondered if you wanna go eat?" Justin asked.

"I want to wash my hair first."

"Do you mind if I go for a walk?"

She shrugged without looking at him.

'What does that mean?' he wondered.

The call from the minarets had stopped not long ago. All good Muslim's would be in the mosques.

'So, by definition, all the bad ones won't,' he rationalised.

"I'm just nipping out then." His comment passed unanswered. "Won't be long," he added from the top of the stairs.

CHAPTER FIFTEEN

D ownstairs there was nobody around. He turned the doorknob and slipped out into the narrow, cobbled, practically deserted alley. He walked to the end and turned left, away from the main square, from the tourist spots.

Soon the stalls changed. Little supermarkets, an Internet cafe, a welding store, a place to get donkey carts repaired replaced the ceramic souvenirs and Marrakech T-shirt stalls.

Justin came to another junction. Overhead, hung between two opposing buildings was a large orange sign. He paused and took a look around to take his bearings for the return journey. Then continued deeper into the labyrinth of narrow streets.

A little further on he spotted what he was searching for. Local youths loitering, two guys standing at the entrance of a dirty old alley looking just as suspicious as any cat would with a whole bucketful of cream.

'Ah-ha.' Justin smiled and headed closer. '*Drug dealers,*' he thought. '*How would the world operate without them?*'

The smaller of the two youths caught Justin's eye and discreetly raised his chin slightly, in an enquiring sort of way.

Justin sort of nodded, and he was already heading towards

them. The dealer moved a little further back into the shadows. He stopped and scratched at a non-existent itch on his shoulder.

'Is this cool?' he asked himself. 'Depends if you wanna get stoned,' came the response.

There wasn't much to say to that. Obviously, the answer was yes, he definitely did. Any logic, the "whys and wherefores" didn't really come into his decision-making process beyond that brief initial scintilla of doubt.

Wearing little more than a smile for protection, he followed the dealer into the shadows.

The second guy ignored him as Justin passed by. He was the tall, silent type. He scoured the crowds, acting as though this whole thing was none of his business. As though he just happened to be standing alongside a drug dealer.

He was surreptitiously checking the crowds for anything untoward. He saw no police, no military, no problems. The people passing by were doing a spectacular job of ignoring him completely. They knew when somebody was up to no good. Bitter experience had taught them it was best to look the other way. They had their own problems. They didn't want to get involved.

Justin casually came alongside his new connection.

The dealer was dressed in a Puma tracksuit and Nike trainers. His hair was gelled back in an impressive dark, lustrous wave, and he wore a solid chunky gold watch on his wrist.

"English?" he asked.

Justin had seen it all before. He'd bought drugs on street corners from London to Lima. He knew how it worked.

The silent, taller guy was the muscle. He probably had a knife tucked up his sleeve.

The smaller one was the salesman. He would possess a smattering of languages. English, French, Spanish, probably Russian and Chinese as well these days. He would be good with numbers, quick at adjusting prices based on how far out of their depth he considered each tourist to be. Most importantly, he was blessed with a killer smile.

"Yes," Justin admitted, "English."

"Cocaina?" the guy asked.

Justin shook his head. "No," he replied, "hashish."

With a skillful shake of the arm, a small piece of hash that must have been up his sleeve appeared in the youth's hand.

Justin smiled. He knew good shit when he saw it.

The dealer smiled back.

"Is it Good?" Justin asked.

He figured they might as well go through the formalities.

"Very good, very soft."

The dealer rolled it between his fingers to verify it was indeed soft and pliable. It buckled like Play-Doh.

"How much for that bit?" Justin asked.

"Four hundred dirham," the youth replied in a flash, the easy smile never once leaving his lips. He offered it across.

Justin took it and squeezed it.

"I'll give you three," he said reluctantly.

"Is very good," came the answer.

"Three hundred," he repeated, pulling exactly three hundred dirham from his pocket and offering it.

The youth beamed.

"Ok," he said, taking the cash. "You come back again, Inglish"

"I will," Justin agreed over his shoulder.

The crowds parted, although not a single one of them acknowledged his sudden presence among them. He strolled calmly away whilst everyone around pretended to be completely unaware a drug deal had just taken place.

CHAPTER SIXTEEN

J ustin climbed the stairs. He was looking forward to a cold drink and a big fat joint. A nice peaceful couple of hours until the heat went out of the sun and then perhaps a stroll around the market square.

It was hot, and his mission was accomplished, it was time to chill.

As soon as he popped his head onto terrace level, Trudy spotted him.

"Where have you been?" she wanted to know. "There's no hairdryer," she added, somehow implying that was important.

"Your hair looks lovely." He smiled at her to show he meant it. *'All women love a compliment,'* he thought.

She took a deep, controlled breath. But before she could reply, Megan appeared.

"We're hungry," said the child. "We wanna go and eat."

Justin frowned. She seemed to be suggesting he adjust his plans to suit other people.

"We're hungry, aren't we, Mummy?" Megan continued.

"You can wait five minutes, can't you?" Justin asked.

The little girl studied him seriously as though considering

his question. "Ok" she agreed, turned on her heel and went to join Malik.

The children had a new game, leaning over the edge of the roof, pointing out cats to each other.

"Why do you need five minutes?" Trudy asked.

He was already dragging out a chair and settling himself at the table.

He pulled a packet of rizla from his pocket.

"Quick joint," he replied.

Trudy said nothing, but if Justin had bothered to look, he might have noticed that she didn't seem best pleased.

"Is there anything to drink?" he asked without looking up.

"Water," Trudy replied sarcastically, meaning there's water in the tap.

"Oh, that would be great," he said. "Could you put some ice in it?"

"Ice?" She sounded incredulous.

Justin looked at her now, for the first time during the whole conversation. "Yeah," he replied. "You could ask the kid or go down to reception." He smiled at her and returned his attention to joint rolling, so he missed the eye roll that nearly tore Trudy's retinas from their sockets.

Once he had lit up and was happily puffing away, Justin's eyes fell across Malik and Megan leaning over the roof.

"Are they ok that close to the edge?" he asked.

Trudy stared at him, struggling to bite her tongue.

He was looking the other way, blissfully unaware that she had taken offence.

"Only you know, best to be safe."

"I think I know what's best for my own daughter," Trudy hissed.

That got his attention. He spun round, and when he saw the look on her face wished he hadn't bothered.

"Yeah, sure," he blustered.

'Seems a little harsh,' he mused. *'Is it safe or not? Only earlier you seemed to think it was a big deal. Just make your mind up, that's all I ask, Jeezus chill girl.'*

He had barely started to calm down, get the full benefit of the drug when Megan let out a scream.

Trudy ran to her daughter. She scooped her up in her arms. Justin ambled over to join them. He thought the better. It seemed like it was the right thing to do. Even though nobody seemed to think it expected of them to give him a bit of peace and quiet, oh no, these kids, they're all me, me, me. *'What about me for a change?'* Justin felt aggrieved.

He squeezed alongside Trudy and joined her in looking over the side of the building. Megan's toy rabbit lay sprawled three stories below. Its limbs and ears twisted at impossible angles. It looked for all the world like a dead body. A small body, a child perhaps.

Justin glanced towards Trudy. He was about to make a comment regarding children playing on the edges of things, but one look at her face and he changed his mind. Only now she knew he was going to say something, now he sort of had to say something.

He blew out a huge puff of smoke and, forcing his expression to remain neutral, asked, "Shall we go eat then?"

'I'll just pretend everything's fine,' he decided. *'It's the English way.'*

Justin took another peek over the edge, so he missed the glare Trudy aimed at him. He also missed her muttered curse, what with the deafening volume of Megan's screams.

"That's the end of the rabbit then," he casually surmised just as Megan paused for breath. They all heard him.

The heartbroken little girl screamed again with renewed vigour. Trudy rolled her eyes so far it actually hurt and somehow managed to keep her opinions to herself.

Justin took her silence as proof she agreed with him. He flicked ash over the side and moved closer to her.

"What's the big deal?" he asked. "It's only a scruffy toy."

"She's had it since the day she was born," Trudy hissed back.

"Oh," he said, and from her tone, he vaguely realised that meant something, and he was supposed to know what. It felt a bit like she was judging him, calling him stupid. He wanted to protest his innocence. He had no children, how was he supposed to know what they did or didn't consider important? But he reluctantly conceded this might not be the appropriate moment.

He went to comfort the distraught child instead.

"It's ok," he assured her, patting her across her little shoulders.

The surprise brought an end to her wailing. She'd never been, what was that, patted like a dog before. She looked into Justin's face.

"Kimmy," she said in a barely audible whisper.

"Who's Kimmy?" Justin was confused now; he thought the issue was the toy.

"Kimmy, my rabbit. You know she's called Kimmy, I told you at the hotel."

"Yeah, yeah, course," he replied.

He recalled her showing him the toys she was bringing on holiday. She'd tipped the whole bagful onto the bed at the most inopportune time if he remembered rightly. That night in the hotel seemed a very long time ago to him now. It was only forty-eight hours.

"We'll get it back," Justin said.

"Her!" Megan screamed.

"Yeah, her, we'll get her back."

The volume in the little girl receded a notch.

"Really?" she eventually spluttered between tears.

"Of course," Justin replied, puffing away. "Just give me some quiet. Let me think."

The child fell silent and looked hopefully up into his face. He'd offered a ray of hope. She was prepared to take anything he had.

He smoked the joint to the roach and threw it over the side. He'd been thinking, but he had nothing.

"Shall we just get another one?"

The screams resumed, turned up a notch.

'This is a nightmare.' He leant over the edge, considered for a split second if he could climb down or send the little boy.

"If only we had a ladder," he said, *'and another spliff,'* he thought.

Megan raced to Malik's side and somehow made him understand that they needed a ladder.

So instead of making another joint, one he badly needed to calm his nerves, by the way, he was being dragged down the stairs and out into the street by a couple of little kids.

Two streets away Malik stopped and pulled a tarpaulin off a ladder.

"Da," he beamed.

"There," Megan declared. "Now we can get Kimmy."

Justin approached the ladder; it seemed rather narrow to him. He half lifted it to test its weight.

"I'm not sure," he said, turning around.

It was then he realised he was talking to himself. The kids had both gone, back to the Riad no doubt. He was expected to retrieve the toy that was bad enough, but he was expected to do so on his own.

'They take the piss, these kids,' he told himself.

An hour later, he re-appeared on the terrace. He'd had a nightmare. A crowd had gathered to watch him scrape his shin, bash his head and get some kind of mould all down his front.

The local populace seemed to find the whole thing highly amusing.

Now he was back, and he had been successful. He expected some serious sympathy.

"Tah-Da!" Justin held out the toy. They didn't have to treat him like a returning hero. Only if they wanted to.

"Mine!"

Megan snatched it from him and ran away.

"You're welcome," Justin called after her.

The four-year-old ignored him totally. She sat on the floor in the shade, talking to her rabbit.

"Did the horrible man hold you by your leg?" she said.

Justin strolled nonchalantly across to Philip.

"Are you hungry?" he asked.

Philip shrugged as his fingers whizzed across the screen of his phone.

Justin looked around.

"Where's your mum?" he asked

Philip shrugged again.

Justin no longer felt like the returning hero. He sat down and rolled himself a joint.

Once he was blowing smoke across the rooftops, he began to feel calmer. Sounds from the bustle of the city below rose up to catch his ear. Spices and bad plumbing combined to assault his nostrils. He tingled with joy, simply at being in Africa.

"This is brilliant, don't you think, Philip?"

Philip shrugged without looking up.

In her little room, Trudy heard him call her name. *'Oh God, he's back,'* she thought.

"Be out in a minute," she called back.

Justin puffed away. *'Probably powdering her nose,'* he decided.

Justin knew the phrase, although he had no idea what it actually meant. What women got up to in private was a complete mystery to him.

'Be positive,' Trudy told herself. *'Megan's made a friend. The sun is shining.'* She was justifying total nonsense to herself. She had to.

She fell back on her yoga and focused on her breathing. She knew how to make herself calm at least to outward appearances if nothing else.

'Appearances are important.' she reminded herself. *'Sometimes you gotta fake it to make it.'*

She'd been faking it all her life, what difference would a few more days make? And it was for the good of Philip and Megan.

Trudy was willing to put on a brave front, to pretend. She had to; if she were to acknowledge reality now, they'd probably cart her off screaming in an ambulance.

She heard Justin say something on the terrace. Not the actual words, just his voice. It made her feel like curling up in a ball on the bed.

'What were you thinking?' she chastised herself for the umpteenth time already that day.

Justin was a complete idiot. That much was obvious. Not only for suggesting this car crash of a trip in the first place, but worse, far worse, he had no social skills at all. How did she not see that before?

'You did,' she reminded herself. *'Lucy made you think you were being ridiculous. Wait 'til I see that girl, she'll not get off lightly for this.'*

"Mummy," Megan was calling from outside.

"Yes, dear?"

"Shall we get Aunty Lucy a tortoise?"

"No, dear."

Trudy clutched her legs tightly, curled up in the foetal position.

. . .

Justin had made another joint. He was halfway through it. He'd discovered that by moving his chair and turning his back on Megan, Malik and Philip, he could block them out, daydream in peace.

'We'll get married in April and take an extended honeymoon, travel the world. It would be just the two of us. Philip is practically old enough to leave home. As for Megan, how expensive can boarding schools be? Everyone says decent schools are better for kids in the long run.'

The mention of Lucy had not helped Trudy's demeanour. Her friend had hinted that maybe this trip would lead to something more serious, wedding bells even.

At this precise moment, the thought of standing at the altar saying "I do" next to Justin made her skin crawl.

Smoking strong hash made Justin lose track of time. Another hour passed before he seriously wondered what was keeping Trudy.

"Shall we go?" he shouted towards her room.

"Comin'," came the reply.

'Does she sound like she's crying?' he asked himself. *'She's fine,'* he decided, stubbing out his joint.

He stood up and prepared to call her again. He didn't need to. She appeared in the doorway, and she looked amazing. He only needed one glance, and Justin was positive she was the one.

Megan was at her mother's side in a flash. "Can we go to the beach?"

They both looked at the child. Justin wasn't going to tell her the nearest beach was miles away. He was saving that information for the right moment.

He stole another glance at Trudy. He couldn't help it; she looked so beautiful.

Trudy felt his eyes on her and looked up. She slid a pair of

Ray-Bans on. From behind them, she took in his dopey puppy dog expression and his bloodshot eyes. She turned away.

"Philip," she said, "we're going to eat. Come on."

The teenager rose to his feet without risking a single glance away from his screen.

"It's a real adventure, isn't it?" Justin asked cheerfully.

Nobody answered. They trooped down the stairs.

For the same reason the widow at a funeral will wear a veil, Trudy made sure she was in front, so nobody could read the expression on her face.

Megan skipped behind her, bouncing the rabbit hard on the handrail with every step. She was singing *'round and round the roses'* to the toy.

She reminded Justin of the title sequence to some blood-soaked, slasher movie. It unnerved him.

Philip, as usual, was on autopilot. He couldn't possibly look at his feet, watch where he was going, because anything of any importance in the world was spinning on the little screen right in front of his eyes and he daren't risk missing a thing.

Justin fell in behind. He was smiling to himself.

'We look like a family,' he mused, and he found the idea rather appealing.

For all intents and purposes, they were a family, he supposed.

He had to acknowledge they weren't exactly close yet, and maybe they didn't communicate all that much, and yes, Trudy seemed quieter than she was in London. So all in all, if he was honest, they did make rather a strange group.

'Don't all families?' he told himself. *'We're normal people just like anyone else.'*

CHAPTER SEVENTEEN

Once they were outside, Justin made a suggestion, "Head to the main square, shall we?"

Trudy sort of smiled, nodded and took Megan by the hand. She hung back, letting Justin lead the way.

'Aww, she's smiling at me again,' he noticed. 'She definitely likes me.'

He was feeling smug. 'She likes me a lot,' he modified his original assumption.

It only took a couple of minutes of navigating the crowded narrow streets, and they were delivered into the wide-open space of the bustling giant square. The scent of garlic and the aromatic smoke of wood burners wafted from tightly packed food stalls across rows of diners seated on hard wooden benches. It was kind of authentic but extremely touristy.

A German couple in smart casual attire found themselves alongside a family of Brits all kitted out in last season's Birmingham City football shirts. The British parents were enquiring rather loudly how much the Germans had paid for their holiday and if booze was included at their hotel.

A pair of rakishly dressed young Italian men engineered it so they were seated across the table from a couple of cute senoritas.

Everybody wanted something they couldn't quite put their finger on. Something special, memorable, quintessentially Moroccan. They were all getting stew, flatbread and Coca-Cola, maybe Fanta orange if they were lucky. And they would all be served before ten pm because at ten-thirty the inspectors would come round handing out fines to any eating establishment that hadn't been stripped bare and moved off the square.

Once the tourists had been fed, the space was needed for the next shift. It was time for the snake charmers, the henna tattooists, and the bag and belt salesmen. But for now, food was on the agenda.

Young men accosted Justin every few yards.

"Here, here," they'd say pointing to an empty cluster of seats.

The phrases "Chicken, mister?" or "Very fresh, very fresh" followed them through the narrow rows of sizzling meat and beautifully displayed salad items. Noises and smells came at them from all directions.

Naturally, Megan added her voice to the affray.

She had released her mother's hand and knew that as long as she stayed within reach, she'd be allowed to retain her freedom. She was already testing the waters, discovering the limits to her independence and pushing them as far as she dare. Not holding hands in a busy crowd she considered devilishly mature. And as an independent young woman, she felt entitled to offer her opinion to the adult world of decision-making.

"This one," she'd say, running to an empty spot at a table and to her delight a young man would appear from nowhere.

"Yes, this one," he'd agree, pulling out chairs, trying to entice them to sit. But every time Justin shook his head and kept moving.

Fortunately, Megan was treating it as a game. She would rush ahead and drape herself over another table,

"This one," she'd plead. "This one."

She seemed to enjoy the sound of the chairs scraping across the floor when the waiters appeared.

After it felt as though they had covered every inch of the giant square and been to every eating establishment available, Trudy could take no more.

"Wait," she called, coming to a halt.

Justin stopped. They all did.

"What are you actually looking for?" she asked him, appearing genuinely mystified.

Justin gave her his best smile. She shuddered.

"I dunno," he said cheerfully. "I guess I'm looking for the perfect place." He moved closer to her and whispered, "When we tell this story to our grandkids, I want everything about it to be perfect."

He stroked her arm, stepped back and beamed. He was absolutely confident she would see what a fabulous plan that was.

"I just want to sit." Trudy was too defeated to respond to his logic, and she sounded it.

"Are you ok?" He didn't understand. Things were going so well.

"I just want to sit," she repeated, and for some inexplicable reason, he hoped she wasn't about to cry.

"This one," he heard Megan shout.

This time Philip had plonked himself down alongside his sister.

"That settles it," Trudy announced as she went and slid onto the bench opposite them.

Justin considered suggesting one more lap of the square, but the waiter was already putting paper napkins and cutlery out for them. Quietly he slid along the bench next to Trudy, so there was that at least.

"Do they do chicken?" asked Megan.

The waiter didn't miss his cue. "Chicken, yes, yes," he said, smiling. "Very tasty, very tasty."

Pretty soon they were all tucking into steaming bowls of stew the waiter claimed was chicken. They were given a plate full of round, flat-bread and a can of Coca-Cola each.

"Is it nice?" Justin said.

"Is this chicken?" Megan asked doubtfully.

"Yes, dear, and it'll make you big and strong."

"The bread tastes funny," Megan replied.

After the meal, they all felt better. They wandered around the giant square for a while. Despite the late hour, there was still an abundance of children, tourists and distractions, the like of which Megan had never seen before. There were cobras in baskets, tortoises and lizards in little wooden cages. A wide variety of garishly coloured plastic tat, none of which would make it past the health and safety executive back in the UK. The stuff was piled high and going cheap.

It was a combination of cheap and cheerful that induced a real carnival atmosphere. And whilst happy punters were more easily parted from their money, large crowds were simple to get lost in.

"Come back, Megan!"

"Hold my hand, Megan!"

"Come back, Megan!"

"Let's just follow her," Justin suggested calmly.

"You're not used to children, are you?"

"Not really," he admitted.

Trudy shook her head. Justin felt like he was being judged, and not in a good way.

When Megan was finally so tired her little legs couldn't manage another step, Justin threw her onto his shoulders, and they headed back.

The square was long ago cleared of eating establishments, and now it had transformed into a giant empty space. Pockets of minimal activity now confined to random patches around the edges, under the few available streetlamps.

'Fertile ground for dealers and pickpockets,' Justin realised.

"This way," he announced.

He took a left turn into an alley, then stopped, doubled back and chose another before scratching his head and starting again.

After a while, Trudy seriously doubted if they'd ever see their beds again. It might be a terrible little room, but at least she could lie down if they could only get there.

Finally, Justin paid a shady looking local to take them back to the Riad.

Little Malik opened the door.

'What's he doing still up?'

Still carrying Megan, Justin took the stairs.

She had been as light as a feather when he'd hoisted for onto his shoulders, she was much heavier by the time he was halfway up the stairs, but he made it to the top and proudly laid her gently on the bed.

Megan wasn't asleep, but neither could she really be described as awake. She was whining. She needed her mother.

"I'll leave you to it," Justin said.

Trudy nodded.

He hadn't given up hope of a snog tonight, but, he reasoned, there was plenty of time for a big fat joint first.

Trudy sang Megan her favourite lullaby until the child was incapable of fighting sleep any longer. Her heavy eyelids fluttered closed, and this time refused to re-open. Trudy waited another five minutes. She was smiling down at her sleeping daughter. She had to admit the day had turned out to be much better than she'd feared. There was no denying that her daughter had thoroughly enjoyed herself. And at the end of the day, isn't that what it was all about?

She rose carefully and tiptoed to the bathroom, still half smiling. She pulled the old-fashioned cord, the light came on, and a dozen cockroaches scattered for their homes in the skirting board.

Trudy screamed. Megan awoke with a start and really screamed.

On the terrace, Justin jumped up so fast his papers, tobacco and hashish fell into the darkness beneath the table. He also, not screamed exactly, but cried out, yelped perhaps, as his shin connected with the heavy iron table leg.

In the adjoining room closeted behind his headphones, Philip's fingers whizzed across his phone. He didn't hear a thing.

"Cockroaches!" Trudy shouted as she emerged from the room clutching her screaming child. "Loads of them! Huge buggers!"

Nobody noticed Malik slip down the stairs.

Megan's screams slowed and stopped dramatically.

"You said 'bugger.'"

"I know, dear."

"What are cocroches?"

She fixed Justin with a withering stare as she explained, "Cockroaches are horrible bugs."

Justin felt the comment seemed aimed at him.

'Nah, it can't be.' Mentally he dismissed such a notion.

"We could buy a spray for them in the morning," he suggested.

Trudy stared at him, her lips pressed tightly together.

"What's the spray do?" Megan wanted to know.

"And in the meantime?" Trudy asked.

Justin had the perfect solution.

"You could sleep in my room," he suggested. "Put Philip in with Megan."

Her lips pressed together so tightly they disappeared from view.

"Malik!" Megan exclaimed as the boy's head appeared at the top of the stairs.

He returned, proudly clutching what seemed to be some kind of cockroach trap. The boy walked solemnly into Trudy's room and plopped his trap in the centre of the bathroom floor. He stood back with his hands on his hips, looking extremely pleased with himself.

You didn't need language to know he thought he'd solved the problem.

Trudy stared aghast, Megan wrapped round her legs.

"What is it, Mummy? What's he doing, Mummy? What's that, mummy?" She reached out to touch it.

"Don't touch it." Trudy pulled her back.

"Why not, Mummy? What is it, Mummy?"

It was at this point Philip chose to make his entrance, still blissfully unaware of the drama he'd missed.

"The wi-fi's gone down," he said. He didn't seem interested that they were all gathered in the tiny bathroom.

Trudy looked at him and burst into tears.

"I can't stay here," she sobbed.

CHAPTER EIGHTEEN

The next day Trudy was up at the crack of dawn. Which meant they all were.

She knocked on the bedroom door, then the window, then sent Megan in to get them out of bed.

"What time is it?" Justin raised his head off the pillow and addressed Megan in a sleepy voice.

"Get up!" she hollered and pulled the blanket off him.

He had a pee, splashed his face with cold water, brushed his teeth, pulled on some shorts and a t-shirt and went to roll a joint.

"There's no time for that," Trudy decreed.

"Huh?"

She didn't answer. Instead, she said, "Philip, let's go."

He appeared, and before Justin was even fully awake, he was following them downstairs.

Trudy hurried them along in double-quick time through the almost empty streets.

Justin couldn't focus, he'd not had a coffee yet, or a spliff. He liked to slowly ease into his days, not start them with a burst of hectic activity. How anyone managed to be out the door early in the morning day after day was a mystery to him.

Finally to Justin's immense relief, Trudy drew to a halt. She was standing in front of a poster depicting a camel train snaking across a golden beach.

"This is the place" Trudy declared. "We passed it yesterday," she added.

Justin was hot from the walk, he didn't really know what he was doing out so early and now something about a camel poster. His head swiveled from Trudy to the poster and back again. It didn't make any sense, she seemed to think it should, but it didn't

"What?" he managed to blurt out.

Megan was inspecting the poster in minute detail.

"Camels," she said. "Look camels."

"Do you want to see the camels?" Trudy asked her.

Immediately the little girl wanted access to the building inside which she assumed they kept the camels advertised on the window.

It was at this point a man came out from what was a travel shop, an excursion bureau? Camel stable? Who knew?

Still, at least he looked pleased to see them. He was smiling broadly. He knew tourists when he saw them.

"Allo," he drew the word out to its limit.

"We want to see the camels," Megan told him.

"Of course," he said. "Come this way."

They all followed Megan into the shop. It was surprisingly small. There was a small desk with a chair either side of it. Megan plopped herself down.

The wallpaper was made up of posters advertising exotic trips.

"Where's the camels?" Megan wanted to know.

"We want to take the trip," Trudy announced.

"Of course," he said. He gestured to a pair of large cushions behind the door. "Would you like to sit?"

Trudy shook her head.

"Chai?" he asked.

"What?" Megan asked.

"Tea, little lady, would you like mint tea?"

She wrinkled her nose and shook her head.

"We just want to book the trip," Trudy said.

"Of course."

He went to his desk and pulled out a brochure.

"We offer two-day or three-day excursions deep into the Sahara desert. A minibus will take you there and meals, accommodation and camel rides will be arranged by real Berber tribesmen. Camel rides," he repeated and gave Megan a wink. She squealed in delight and wriggled in the chair.

The salesman finished his spiel, "All are included in the price."

Trudy made the arrangements like a woman in a hurry. When the time came to pay, Justin stepped forward.

"How much?" he asked, pulling out his wallet.

"Twelve hundred dirham."

Justin counted out the money and handed it over. The notes disappeared somewhere in the man's robes.

"We leave in one hour," he informed them. "From the bus stop in the main square."

"Got it," Trudy said and was already heading for the door.

Justin waited, expecting some form of proof of the transaction. He'd been given no tickets, no receipt, no nothing.

Trudy poked her head around the door. "Come on," she said. "We should go and pack."

Justin's eyes darted between the salesman and the door.

"Tickets?" he said, holding out his hand.

"One hour," the man told him. "The bus stop in the square."

Megan banged on the window.

"Ok," Justin caved. "One hour."

"Yes, yes."

So far, Justin was finding the day rather stressful.

He left without trying to get any sense out of the guy.

"Could we find somewhere to get a coffee?" he begged Trudy.

"The coach leaves in one hour," she reminded him.

Justin understood she was denying his request.

Back at the hotel, breakfast was being served on the roof. There was warm bread and fresh fruit, hot coffee and sweet pastries. Some of the other guests were tucking in. Justin went to join them.

"We don't have time," Trudy reminded him.

"We're going to the beach," Megan informed Malik.

He smiled and nodded as though he understood. In one hand he held the baby tortoise, in his other hand half an apple.

The two children sloped away from the breakfast table so they could feed their pet in peace.

Justin went to his room, threw his toothbrush and some underwear in a bag, and he was ready.

Regardless of Trudy's rules, he went to sit down. There had to be time for a coffee and a joint.

Justin had eaten some bread and jam. Now he sat on the terrace smoking and drinking coffee, watching the kids sharing pieces of fruit with a tortoise. He wasn't sure they should be eating bits of apple from the floor, but neither was he sure they'd pay any attention to him.

"I think Mummy's calling you," he said to Megan. "It might be about the camels."

She went to see.

'Kids are so easy to manipulate.' Justin put that one down as the closest to a victory he'd got all morning.

As Megan disappeared into the bedroom, he heard her ask, "What about the camels?"

"What, dear?"

"Why have you got my toothbrush, Mummy?"

"I'm packing for you."

"Have you got my swimming costume?"

"Yes."

"Can I bring my tortoise?"

"No."

"Please, Mummy. He'll be good."

'Perhaps it was this constant demand for attention that was stressing Trudy out.'

Justin topped up his coffee just as Trudy appeared in the doorway.

"Coffee?" he asked. He was more than willing to pour her a cup.

"No time," she said before disappearing back in the room.

She made him feel he'd done something wrong. Could he have offended her? The thought crossed his mind for a split second. He shook his head.

'Nah, that's ridiculous,' he told himself. *'You're just being paranoid. She's on holiday. Of course she's ok.'*

He relaxed until she emerged again, this time dragging a holdall.

"Want me to take that?" Justin offered.

He regretted his kindness as soon as he attempted to shoulder the bag. He'd seriously underestimated how much you could get in these things.

"Wanna take your mum's bag for a bit?" he asked Philip.

The teenager glanced at the bag, then back to his phone. He didn't bother to answer.

Trudy led the way to the square. She took a wrong turning, so they had to retrace their steps slightly. So, by the time they got to the bus the other passengers were already aboard. Fortunately, despite the lack of paperwork, the driver was clearly expecting them. He hadn't expected to wait for them perhaps, but they were here now.

Apart from four seats on the back row for the English latecomers, the bus was full.

Once they were seated and Justin had an opportunity to give his fellow passengers the once over, he noticed that Megan was the only child aboard. It was a mainly retired bunch gathered together from all points of the European continent.

Once the bus was moving, Megan left her seat and roamed up and down the aisle making friends. In the main, the tourists were happy to play along. But leaning across people and shaking hands with a little English girl was a novelty the other passengers quickly got bored of.

She returned to her seat, no doubt plotting her next move, Justin figured.

A couple of hours into the journey, there was an announcement over the tannoy. It came in German first, then French, and finally English.

"Comfort break, Ladies and Gentlemen. Please be back in your seats in twenty minutes; we've a long way to go."

'At last,' Trudy thought.

She hadn't been willing to brave the cockroach-infested bathroom. She'd been holding on for hours.

"Keep an eye on her while I find a toilet?" she asked.

Justin nodded, smiled, "No problem."

"Stay with Justin," she told her daughter.

Megan nodded.

Trudy was off the coach the moment the doors opened.

Megan sat patiently as instructed. Until, that is, Justin turned away. Then she was up and scuttling through the legs of the other passengers. All he could do was watch her disappear.

He shuffled down the bus painfully slowly whilst through the windows he watched Megan approach and immediately befriend a group of Moroccan children.

By the time he'd descended the steps and hit the ground, she was nowhere in sight.

He was defeated before he'd even begun.

Philip, seemingly oblivious to his missing sister, came alongside Justin in the car park. "Thank God," Justin heard him mutter as he passed. "Wi-fi." The teenager found a seat in the cafe whilst attacking his phone with renewed vigour.

Justin was torn between joining the food queue and searching for Megan. He really wanted a coffee, but he felt sure Trudy would want to know where her daughter was.

He actually took a few paces towards the queue before some deep primal instinct got the better of him and he went to look for her.

"Megan!" he called from the door.

"Megan!" he called a little louder as he headed around the back of the cafe.

She appeared almost immediately. Bizarrely her T-shirt was wrapped around her head and looked to be soaking wet. She was being trailed by a pack of children, some of whom also wore T-shirts over their heads.

"Ah, there you are." He was relieved that finding her had proved to be so easy. "Don't disappear."

She looked him right in the eye, laughed in his face and ran off with her posse right behind her. They disappeared around one side of the cafe a split second before Trudy appeared from the other direction.

Justin smiled at her. He took a few steps back and tried to see if the kids were still in view. They weren't.

"Where's Megan?" the question came before he was ready. It seemed a bit unfair, a little ambushy.

"Oh, she's fine."

"Fine?"

"Yeah, she's just playin' over there." He pointed vaguely to his left. "Do you fancy a coffee?"

She nodded, but her brow was furrowed, she seemed a little suspicious. She took a few steps towards where he'd pointed.

"I'll get us some coffee then?"

Trudy nodded whilst scanning the area for her daughter.

Justin slipped into the cafe.

When he returned, the pack of kids were still nowhere to be seen.

"She still playing?" he asked.

"She came and ran off again."

"She'll be back."

"I know," Trudy agreed.

'Thank god for that.'

He moved towards her, conscious it was just the two of them.

The giant African sun beat down from an impossibly blue sky. The wild Atlas Mountains stretched out around them as far as the eye could see.

"Nice spot for a coffee, eh?" he ventured, handing her one.

It could have been a romantic moment, a shared experience to draw them closer together. But it wasn't. Neither of them had anything to say that might be of interest to the other.

Justin thought they must share numerous common interests. He just needed to uncover what they were.

Trudy wasn't a child so she knew there could never be any spark, any future between such polar opposites.

They stood sipping their coffee like two strangers thrown together at a funeral.

"Awkward" didn't begin to cover it. Those far-off dates in the trendy districts of London seemed a lifetime ago when viewed from here in the mountains.

"I wouldn't mind a smoke," she said. "You know, for the bus ride."

He didn't need to be asked twice.

"Good idea." He beamed but mainly just because he was

pathetically grateful she'd broken the silence. Getting stoned would take the edge of her stress levels he figured.

As Justin rolled a joint, she could see Philip in the cafe. Well, she could see a bit of his left shoulder.

Megan and her newfound friends were chasing a dog around the café. They would appear then disappear.

For a while, all was at peace with the world.

Justin allowed himself to fantasize as he rolled. He imagined them growing old and happy together.

For her part, Trudy, for the first time that day, didn't feel like killing him.

Things may not yet be perfect, but it was a definite step in the right direction.

Two joints later they were back on the bus and rattling across the badly surfaced roads.

Trudy was definitely more docile. Justin rested his hand on her thigh. She ignored it. He took that as a good sign.

It was dark before the bus stopped again.

That night they slept in a giant Bedouin tent somewhere on the coast.

There was only one blanket each, and the temperature hit freezing in the middle of the night.

Justin imagined he was a Berber tribesman.

Trudy felt every inch the city girl. She felt like crying she was so cold. She was clinging tightly to Megan hoping for body warmth, but it seemed to be a one-way street. Her daughter slept soundly wrapped in her mother's ice-cold arms.

She thought the morning would never come.

It was difficult to tell where Philip stood on the situation. His face was hidden beneath his hood.

CHAPTER NINETEEN

The next day a tortoise again bit Megan at breakfast.

Justin couldn't help wondering if it was a complete coincidence.

She allegedly hadn't spotted it on the floor, and when it tried to suck a tiny piece of apple from her toe, she went ballistic.

Fruit and croissants went somersaulting into the air. A glass coffee pot tipped and rolled onto the lap of an immaculately turned-out German tourist.

In the end, Justin had to sneak off for a joint just to calm his nerves.

This trip, though, was different from what he was used to. Megan seemed able to turn anything into a drama. It was exhausting.

By the time he returned to the breakfast table, all had been dealt with. The waiter had sliced an apple into little pieces. Megan was now feeding it to the tortoise.

"They eat flies too," the waiter told her.

This was fascinating news indeed. She went off armed with a fly squatter.

Philip had a wi-fi connection. Megan was busy hunting flies.

All was peaceful in the world.

As Justin sat, he nodded politely at the German man jabbering away. He didn't understand a word.

He reached for the coffee pot.

As he tipped, still nodding politely, the lid came off.

The last of the coffee rushed across the table into the lap of the same German woman who had been on the receiving end before.

She shrieked and jumped to her feet. With his hood up and his headphones on, Philip didn't see her flailing arm until it was too late.

The Frau caught him squarely across the nose.

Blood began to gush almost instantly.

The coach trip was delayed whilst Philip was taken to the local pharmacy.

The mainly German crowd was polite enough not to blame the English openly.

The guide offered to take Philip to be patched up.

"I should go as well," Trudy decided.

Justin nodded.

"Are you goin' to be ok?"

"We'll be fine, Mummy," Megan assured her.

"Yeah, I'll look after her," Justin added.

Trudy actually rolled her eyes.

She turned to Megan. "Be good, darlin'," she said, kissed her on the forehead and they were gone.

CHAPTER TWENTY

The cab driver told Justin it would take one hour to get to the pharmacy, be seen and come back.

Naturally, Justin intended to take his responsibilities seriously.

He may not have much experience with children, but he was the adult. These things came naturally, didn't they? Otherwise, how had the human race managed to survive for so long? She wouldn't get away from him as easily as she had at the cafe. She'd taken an unfair advantage that time. Things were going to be different from now on.

He looked down at her a little dubiously.

She smiled sweetly back.

"Shall we go and get a coffee?" he suggested.

She turned up her little nose. "I don't drink coffee," she stated, apparently amused by such a thought.

"Ice cream, I mean," he corrected himself. "Shall we get an ice cream?"

She nodded. She allowed Justin to take her hand, and they joined the crowds milling up and down the main street, the only street.

They found a cart selling flavoured ices. The vendor made an almighty fuss of Megan. He complimented Justin on his adorable little girl in excellent English.

As they walked in the hot sun eating their ice creams, Justin began to reassess.

'*Actually being a parent is quite good fun,*' he decided, completely contradicting his stance on the subject over the last few days. They wandered aimlessly onto the sandy beach.

Powerful surf was rolling in. A group of noisy children were playing on the tide line. As each wave crashed ashore, they screamed with delight and tried not to get wet.

Megan watched transfixed, licking her ice cream.

It certainly looked like a lot of fun. Once her ice was gone, inevitably she asked, "Can I go play with them?"

"Sure," he smiled. Delighted to be able to grant her request. To be able to earn a few extra brownie points.

She skipped down the golden sand and very soon was caught up in the action.

Justin thought he should do the grown-up thing and make sure the other kids played nice. He sat up straight and watched her diligently. He needn't have worried. She had clearly been accepted into the fold like a long-lost friend and was soon running up and down the wet sand, screaming along with the best of them.

Justin relaxed. He rested back on his elbows and closed his eyes for a moment relishing the warmth on his face, the feeling of being on holiday.

After a few minutes, he knew he should check on Megan so sat up and looked down the beach. He immediately saw her running and laughing. He slumped down again and let the sun warm his skin.

Forty-five minutes later, that was where Trudy found him.

"What are you doin'?"

He recognised the voice instantly. He opened his eyes. Sure enough, there she was standing over him.

Justin smiled. "Hi," he said.

Trudy wasn't smiling.

"Where's Megan?" she demanded.

'Oh shit!'

Quickly he sat up to point her out amongst the group of children. Only things looked different for some reason. The sea was still there, albeit a bit closer, but there were no kids, not one.

"Where is she?" he said.

"What?" Trudy demanded.

Justin smiled sheepishly. "Well…" he began.

"Is that her?" Philip asked.

He pointed far away down the sandy beach where giant cliffs rose majestically to the road above. Waves were crashing into the base of the rock and whooshing out of a blowhole high above the sand.

A group of children, little more than small dots, could be seen risking their lives. Taking it in turns to cling onto the rock and let waves soak them whilst hoping not to be dislodged.

Even from this distance, Trudy could see one of the little girls didn't look local. "That's her." To Justin's ear she sounded cross.

"Nothing to worry about then," Justin offered brightly. "She's fine."

"She's halfway up a bloody great mountain, and she can't swim," Trudy hissed through gritted teeth.

She didn't add, 'You were supposed to be watching her.' She didn't need to. It was implied in the filthy look she threw him.

"Oh," he replied. "I'll go fetch her, shall I?"

Justin ran as fast as his legs would carry him. He had to if he wanted to get there first; Trudy was right behind him.

"Megan, come down," he called from the base of the cliff.

One or two of the children spared him a fleeting glance. Megan wasn't one of them. If he wanted her attention, he would need to get closer.

He'd never really been much of a climber, but Trudy was hot on his heels, and he realised she was expecting it. So rather than wait to be given the order, he put his hands to the cliff face and began to ascend.

It was a long way up, although Justin was covered in sweat long before reaching any dizzy heights.

"Megan," he hissed whilst clinging on tightly.

This got the attention of the nearest children. They started sniggering, jabbering in Moroccan and pointing at him. He had no idea what was so funny.

"Megan," he hissed again, slightly louder.

This time she looked. She too burst into laughter.

"What's so funny?"

"You look like a zebra," she stated.

Justin had no idea he'd been dozing beneath a slated piece of wood. Half his face had turned a violent shade of red, in neat symmetrical lines.

"Come down!"

Megan scooted away from him, sending loose rocks rolling to the beach as she did so.

"Come here!" he shouted. "Mummy wants you."

She laughed.

"I'm serious!"

Megan laughed again and hid behind a little girl who was also laughing and pointing at him.

Justin grimaced.

'I'm the grown-up here.'

He forced himself to climb a little higher.

'Just a bit more and I can grab her.'

The angry wave rushed out of the blowhole with a watery whoosh.

All the kids laughed and screamed and jumped nimbly away from it.

Justin stared openmouthed. He'd been caught in no man's land. He closed his eyes a split second before it crashed over him. He kept them closed and bumped down the solid, unforgiving rock. Then lay at the bottom, seeing stars through his eyelids whilst discretely flexing muscles. Examining himself for broken bones.

"Are you ok?"

Trudy's soft voice broke through his pain.

"It'll take more than that…"

The sentence remained unfinished because a stone landed inches from his head.

The children on the cliff were not at all sympathetic to his predicament. They were gathering up stones as fast as they could and pelting him. It was nothing personal, just high jinks.

He retreated smartly, proving no bones were broken.

Finally, Trudy managed to coax her daughter down.

CHAPTER TWENTY-ONE

J ustin tried not to limp too much as they started the walk back to town. On the main street, they passed a street vendor selling crepes.

"Can I have one, Mummy?" Megan asked.

There was a cardboard sign offering Nutella as one of the toppings.

"With Nutella," Megan added as her eyes fell on the picture of something she actually recognised.

"We'll all have one, shall we?" Justin suggested.

There was nowhere to sit down. They were forced to eat where they stood. Justin's leg throbbed, but he chose to suffer on silence. He wasn't sure how much sympathy he'd receive and didn't want to risk disappointment.

As they ate, two little girls approached, one with her hands cupped. They looked as though they had been walking across the Sahara for days their clothes were so dusty. The oldest was about seven years old. She came to a halt in front of Justin.

"Meester," she repeated over and over with her hands cupped.

Justin felt awful. Not because poverty upset him. But

because his head was still spinning from falling off the rocks and because the flies wouldn't leave the cut on his leg alone.

He shook his head; still the beggar persisted.

"No," he barked at her firmly before continuing to nibble at his still too hot crepe. He looked away.

With hindsight, he realised he shouldn't have taken his eyes off her, but that's why hindsight is such a wonderful thing.

He felt something on his hip and glanced down to see the beggar trying to put her hand in his pocket.

"Fuck off!" he yelped, jumping back.

Nobody else had seen what just happened.

"Don't speak to her like that," Trudy snapped at him.

"She was trying to pick my pocket." He was indignant.

"Don't be ridiculous."

"She was," he insisted.

"What is wrong with you?"

"She was trying to rob me."

Trudy shook her head in pity. "It's sad," she told him.

"I swear..."

"Just leave it, will you," Trudy muttered. She was speaking in a tone designed not to frighten the children.

"Everyone's getting back on the bus," said Philip.

Trudy tried to think of a reason not to get on; she wasn't looking forward to a long drive.

"Camels!" screamed Megan as she pushed past Justin in her haste to climb the steps.

"Ouch, my leg!"

The comfort break, the sun and the motion of the bus soon caused most of the elderly passengers to start nodding off.

Justin managed to squeeze himself into the corner of the back seat and finally get some rest.

Philip played with his phone whilst Trudy entertained Megan.

By the time the bus stopped and Justin awoke, he was feeling much better.

"Are we there yet?" Megan asked above the hiss of hydraulic brakes.

"Not yet, dear."

There came an announcement over the tannoy. They waited for the English translation. "We hope you enjoyed your trip. If so, there is a plate by the door as you exit. Feel free to show your appreciation for the driver."

By the time the English version finished they were the only remaining passengers aboard.

"It seemed much longer in German," Trudy noted.

Justin shrugged.

As they disembarked, Trudy felt obligated to drop a few coins into the hat. It was the least she could do after her daughter's antics.

Megan was standing on a stone wall, hands on hips, surveying her surroundings.

"I can't see any camels," she announced, not bothering to hide her disappointment.

A local man in a flowing robe hissed to catch her attention.

"Camels, this way," he said in English.

"This way, Mummy," Megan called over her shoulder already racing towards the stranger.

"Camels?" the man addressed his question at Justin, who nodded.

"Over there," he pointed to a jeep.

Most of the other passengers from their bus were sitting at tables, clearly expecting food and drink; a few were climbing aboard the dusty yellow jeep.

"More travelling?" Philip asked.

"Camels," the man repeated and pointed once again.

Soon they were moving across the Sahara in an open-topped

jeep. Bouncing around so much that conversation was impossible.

Justin had to admit it was making him forget about his rock-climbing injuries.

Trudy had her teeth tightly clenched. It was the only way she could stop them clattering together.

The phrase "I'm trapped in Hell" played over and over in her mind.

Megan was unaffected by the discomfort. She bounced in her seat like the excited toddler she was.

"I can't see them yet," she said.

"There's no trees," she observed.

"Still can't see any," she informed them every thirty seconds.

"There's no wi-fi," Philip mumbled inaudibly.

His mother shrugged.

"Will they have wi-fi when we get there?" he wanted to know.

"I don't know, dear," she told him.

They were on the very top of a giant dune. In all directions, as far as the eye could see, there was nothing but fine, golden sand. No trees, no plants of any description. No buildings, not even a solitary rock, just sand, sand and more sand. It was barren, desolate, and hauntingly beautiful.

Eventually, the jeep tipped forwards and started its ascent.

"Look, Megan!" Trudy pointed.

Far below camels were rising to their feet. Megan bounced excitedly as she saw them.

She was ecstatic and wanted everybody to know it.

"Look, Mummy!" Much tugging at Trudy's arm.

"Yes, dear, I see them."

"Look, Philip!"

He snatched his arm away after the first tug.

"Camels!" she screamed at Justin, and he wondered if his ears would ever stop ringing.

Through the heat haze, the animals lazily lurched to their feet and, under the direction of the herder's whip, formed into a curving line.

Being an open-topped vehicle, Megan's high-pitched screams weren't restricted to the interior of the jeep. Instead, they echoed off the natural amphitheatre of the dunes. She loved that; it encouraged her to go louder.

Trudy thought her head would explode.

Finally, they reached the bottom, and the screams faded away.

Trudy had never been so grateful.

"I'll just wait here," she said.

"No, Mummy."

The little girl dragged her mother over for a closer look.

"Look how big they are." Trudy had never been this close to a camel before.

The Berber herdsman saw how she eyed his creatures. He'd encountered beginner's nerves before. He also had an eye for a pretty girl.

"You take number one camel? Very safe, I will lead you personally."

She still looked doubtful.

"I have great experience," the desert nomad proudly declared, pointing to his chest as though that was the end of the matter.

She had to admit he looked the part with his deeply ingrained tan, flowing robes and traditional headscarf.

"Ok," she reluctantly agreed.

"What's his name?" Megan asked.

"Rafael," he told her.

"Hello, Rafael." She was already stroking its nose.

"Is it ok to touch him?" Trudy asked warily.

"Yes, yes, he very friendly. He likes little girls."

Megan liked the sound of that.

"Do you think he likes me?" she wanted to know.

"Here." the man came over to her and gently took her hand. "Stroke him here, like this. He likes this. Not like this." He reverted to what she had been doing. "Like this" he switched back again. "If you do that he likes you for sure."

Megan beamed and continued the motion on her own after he stepped back.

The man looked at Trudy. "Wait here," he told her, and wrapping his robes around him, he went to organise the rest of his other customers. Trudy could wait. She would be last in the saddle. He always gave the nervous ones the least amount of time to chicken out.

He stopped at every camel all the way to the end of the train. Shared a few words here, checked stirrup fastenings there, joked with the old woman traveling alone. All the time he, was switching easily from one language to another. He didn't seem to be in much of a hurry. Nobody was. Except Megan, who could barely contain herself by the time he finally got back to them and hoisted Trudy up. And with Megan perched precariously on her lap, the train set off.

Their camel was wearing a harness, attached to which was a length of rope. The other end was firmly in the hand of the Berber. Trudy began to relax. She looked behind and saw her son was not where he should be.

Instantly any feelings of calm evaporated.

Philip should have been directly behind her, but he wasn't. Instead, she was looking at a young German tourist. One who'd gone to a lot of effort to go part-time native. Not only did he have a traditional scarf wrapped around his head, he'd also splashed out for the robes. Well, a touristy version of Berber robes that he'd probably picked up in Marrakech market. Clearly, he fancied himself as some kind of Lawrence of Arabia.

Around his neck was a big, solid Pentax camera. He intended

to document this trip of a lifetime, and no doubt bore his friends and family about it for months after returning home.

Then Trudy saw Philip on the camel after him. It turned out the camels preferred to line up this way around, and nobody had told her of the change of plans.

Behind Philip were a smattering of tourists mostly wearing Berber headscarves from the gift shop and looking quite pleased with themselves. Finally, bringing up the rear was Justin.

He had watched Trudy wobble as her camel moved and how tightly she was clinging onto Megan and had feared the worst. He tried to keep his eye on them. But as the path twisted through the dunes, they inevitably were lost from sight.

He left them to it and concentrated on his own ride.

It was great.

He began to relax, to think.

Just as he convinced himself he'd mastered riding the ship of the desert, his camel ploughed through the lip of a particularly steep dune and tilted violently forwards. With Justin clinging to its neck, the camel began to drop down the other side. Justin held on tight and managed to avoid catastrophe.

The camel delivered him safely up and down a few more dunes before his confidence fully returned. Only then did he risk peeking ahead trying to pick out Trudy.

At the front of the train, he just about picked out a figure leading a camel. They were so far ahead he forgot about them. Concentrated on enjoying his ride instead. This was, after all, something he may never get the chance to experience ever again.

And what an experience it was, what magnificent beasts they truly were! He felt like an action hero in an adventure novel. He loved the way the beast lolled from side to side, whilst simultaneously tipping its great bulk back and forth as it navigated the endless dunes.

'To think they've been carrying man across this very sand for hundreds of years.' It blew his mind.

He pretended to be Indiana Jones. He fantasized all the way to the designated rest stop.

"That was brilliant!" he announced as he climbed off.

He was beaming at Trudy, at Megan, at the back of Philip's head. None of them returned his enthusiasm.

"Wasn't it?" he added with the excitement in his voice turned down a notch.

"Mummy got blood on her," Megan replied.

"No, she didn't," Justin answered in a jokey voice as though such a thing was ridiculous.

Trudy turned around, and there was indeed a red splatter across her back. It was difficult to tell whether it was blood, though.

"That's not blood," he blurted out confidently, in a tone of disbelief.

Both females stared at him, Megan frowning, Trudy looking aghast. Even Philip gave Justin a shake of the head as though to signify there was no helping some people, before disappearing without a word back beneath his hood.

"It's camel blood," Megan declared.

'At least it's not human,' he was tempted to say but decided against it.

"How do you get camel blood all the way up your back?" he said instead.

"All the way up my back?" This sounded as though it was news to Trudy.

"On your back" he corrected himself, but it was too late, she was already pulling her top off.

He couldn't help staring.

'Mmmm, black lace bra,' he thought. *'Focus,'* he chastised himself and was feeling just guilty enough to avert his gaze.

"Oh, bloody hell!" Trudy muttered as she inspected the

soiled item.

"From a camel," Megan replied, still mentally juggling with his daft question. "You get camel blood from a camel."

"Yes, yes." Justin smiled sarcastically to show he knew that. "But how did it manage to bleed on Mummy?"

"It wasn't the one she was riding, silly."

'How am I the silly one here,' he wondered, knowing full well it was a moot point.

Megan pointed to the German tourist who'd been on the second camel.

"He dropped his camera an' tried to save it. He made his camel push ours, so ours kicked his in the face. It shook its head, and all this blood sprayed everywhere an' some went on Mummy. It was his fault."

She pointed again at the young German whose very expensive camera had just been swallowed up by sand, never to be seen again. He didn't look that happy.

Megan raised her eyebrows. "I wasn't scared at all." She wanted to make that clear before shrugging in a 'what you gonna do?' kind of way. It was adorable.

They made the most of a picnic in the desert, but Trudy was dreading the return trip so much she couldn't eat. Whilst Megan couldn't rest, she was impatient to get riding again.

Trudy wanted to have total concentration if she was going to climb back on the giant beast. So Megan climbed up with Justin, an arrangement that made Trudy a little happier, so naturally he was happy to agree.

There was genuine pleasure to be had from witnessing Megan's joy and all he had to do was hold on to her tightly. It sort of confirmed his suspicion that parenthood was far easier than people claimed.

Megan had completely worn herself out by the time they climbed on to the bus to Marrakech.

She slept almost from the moment they pulled away.

CHAPTER TWENTY-TWO

When they returned to the hotel, Philip was straight on his phone and could not be contacted any other way. Trudy took Megan to the room to prepare her for bed. Justin had some time to himself.

He slumped down on the cushions around the iron table and rolled himself a big, fat joint.

He considered getting up to admire the view of the city, but his body was aching after the day's punishment, he didn't want to stand. He contented himself with sitting there, listening to the sounds of the city.

He was smoking his third joint before anyone joined him. Megan appeared first. "There was hot water," she announced cheerfully.

"That's good," Justin answered.

Trudy appeared shortly after her daughter. To Justin, she looked like a freshly scrubbed movie star.

"The hot waters made you both shiny?" he observed.

Megan looked herself up and down. Then did the same to her mother. "Mummy's hair is nice and shiny," she agreed. Her innocence was sweet.

Megan had thoroughly enjoyed her day. She went to bed willingly for a change, on the understanding that tomorrow was going to be just as much fun.

She fell asleep as soon as she hit the pillow.

Trudy came to join him on the cushions; she even took a few tokes of his super loaded joints.

'This is it,' he told himself. 'This is your moment, say something cute damn you!'

"I'm sorry," he said, "about today." He passed her a joint like some kind of peace offering.

She hesitated briefly, took it, looked him right in the eye and smiled.

"Ok"

'Hallelujah!' he thought. 'We can start again. From here.'

Justin was relieved she hadn't pressed him specifically on what he was apologising for. He didn't want to make a list. What if he missed something out she considered a big deal? A blow-by-blow dissection of the beach incident wasn't going to help anyone.

Trudy inhaled deeply before blowing a cloud of smoke out into the night. Then she turned to face him and asked, "What are you apologising for?"

"Eh?" he was thrown.

She let him squirm for a minute then half smiled to show she was teasing him.

"Should I just accept the apology and move on?" she gently suggested.

He nodded gratefully.

She touched the back of his hand. "You're forgiven."

Her touch sent sparks racing through his arm, his groin, his mind.

'This is it,' he thought. He began to lean in for a kiss.

"Mummy?"

A little voice dimmed the magic somewhat. "I'm not sleepy

now." Megan appeared. She crawled across the cushions climbed into her mother's lap.

"Have you seen Yaya?"

"What?" Justin asked.

"My tortoise," she explained.

"Go to bed," Trudy said.

"Are we going to the beach tomorrow?"

"If you go to bed we might."

She considered this for a moment and, seemingly satisfied, crawled off her mum. They watched her cross the tiles. She stopped at the bedroom door and turned to face them,

"Night night, Mummy, I had a lovely day," she said.

"You're welcome, darling," Trudy answered happily.

"I'm going to bed now," she explained for Justin's benefit.

"Night night," Justin said.

"Where were we?" Justin said once they were alone.

"I'll see you in the morning." Trudy rose. "I'm tired. I wanna make sure she's ok."

Not even a peck on the cheek.

"Night then," he said, sounding a little disappointed.

He stayed up alone and got really stoned.

CHAPTER TWENTY-THREE

The next day Justin overslept. By the time he surfaced from his pit, the others had all gone out.

He ordered some coffee from the reception and set about to enjoy a lazy morning smoking dope and reading his book.

At lunchtime, he went out for a snack shortly before they came back. By the time he returned they'd gone again.

It wasn't until late afternoon they caught up with each other.

Trudy appeared at the top of the stairs looking refreshed, radiant and beautiful.

"You look great," he told her.

"Thanks."

She was laden down with grocery bags and looked so good he went to help.

"You've been shopping."

"Yes," Megan said. "We've got tomatoes, cucumber, crab meat, and what else have we got, Mummy?"

"Justin will put it all out on the table. Then you can see," she answered with a smile. "Is that ok?"

"Will he make it ready?" She sounded suspicious.

"No, I will, dear, is that ok?"

By way of reply, she nodded and went to sit at the table.

"Empty the bags then," she ordered.

"Of course."

What else could he say?

They had an evening in. Philip on his phone, Trudy preparing then clearing away the meal, and Megan playing quietly with Malik while Justin smoked dope.

The trials and tribulations of yesterday were left in the past. They presented a rooftop scene of domestic bliss. This was what Justin considered a holiday.

Trudy obviously agreed. After a while, she came and sat beside him. His hopes arose. He wasn't to know she looked so relaxed because she'd just had a day without him.

Trudy had barely settled down when, "I'm going to bed now," Megan announced.

It was so unexpected her mother instinctively checked her watch.

"Excuse me?" she queried.

"I'm going to bed now, I'm tired."

"I'll come and tuck you in," Trudy offered not really wanting to get up so soon after sitting down.

"That's ok, Mummy, I've cleaned my teeth." She padded over and breathed on her to prove the point.

"You don't usually go to bed on your own." Trudy was confused.

"Yes, I do."

Her daughter glanced across at Justin, and Trudy realised this was some kind of stance about being a grown-up and making her own decisions.

"Ok." She smiled and kissed her on the nose.

Megan scampered away.

As they watched her go, Justin allowed his hand to wander into Trudy's. She didn't pull away, but neither did her fingers curl around his.

"I should go an' tuck her in," she said. Clearly, he didn't yet have her undivided attention.

And something about her tone gave Justin cause for concern. They were close; he didn't want her to get distracted now.

"She'll be fine," he replied. "She's only there. You can see the door. There's no other way out."

She wiggled her nose which meant, "I'm not sure."

"We'll snuggle up and watch over that door like US Marines," he suggested, emphasising the "snuggle up" part of the plan.

"Well," she began, as though she was considering it.

He dared hope.

Then she pushed him away.

"I'll just go check on her."

She smiled sweetly, acknowledging his disappointment. But the magic was gone. It would have to be built back up. He felt deprived although he perked up watching her walk across the terrace.

'What a body, she's worth the wait. We've got all night.'

Justin was immediately lost in thought. He didn't realise he was grinning.

'Ah, this is the life!'

It took a scream to bring him back to reality. A loud, female scream.

He wasn't sure whether it was Trudy or Megan. Then it came again.

'That's Trudy,' he decided. He was equally concerned with whether he had guessed correctly than with what the screaming was about.

He did deem it worthy of investigation.

As he got to his feet, a cat came flying from the girl's room. By the time he had sauntered halfway across the terrace, more had followed it.

They moved fast, and they kept on coming, so it was hard to be sure, but he thought he counted five.

He got to the bedroom just as Trudy staggered into the doorway.

"She brought a bloody fish back from the beach!"

'She's hysterical,' he thought. *'I shouldn't say hysterical. Girls don't like to be called hysterical,'* he checked himself, nodded slightly as though agreeing with her but really because he'd made a deal with himself. *'Is it ok to say it to yourself?'* he wondered.

"And she's been enticing cats in with it!" Trudy roared.

'Surely it's ok if she is actually being hysterical?' he allowed.

"What?" he offered all he had.

"A bloody fish!" She glared at him. "Cats!" she hissed, and he got the feeling it was his fault. It wasn't at all romantic.

It was as if he was the one who had filled the bedroom with cats. He was tempted to object.

'You're hysterical,' he said, but just to himself.

"Do you know where she got the fish from?"

He decided not to offer any guesses.

"When she was at the beach with you," she spat out.

To Justin, it felt as though she wasn't letting those sleeping dogs lie. Even though, technically, they had agreed to put it behind them.

He consoled himself by calling her hysterical again. But obviously not out loud, where it was safe to do so, privately.

As it turned out, he didn't need to answer. They were interrupted by another scream.

This was also female in origin but came from a much younger source.

'That was Megan,' he guessed, resisting the urge to smile, that one was too easy.

Who else could it be? It even came from her room.

Megan came to the door, awkwardly clutching a disgruntled cat.

"He scratched me," she declared.

"Put him down!" Trudy shouted.

The cat wriggled furiously. Megan dropped it but not before getting another scratch down the whole length of her left arm.

"He scratched me again!" she howled.

"Leave him!" Trudy ordered.

"I've got fur in my mouth," Megan screamed, and the realisation sent her completely batshit.

CHAPTER TWENTY-FOUR

The hospital was spotless.

Justin glanced towards Trudy.

"See," he said. "It's fine."

She sort of nodded. Kind of acknowledged he'd been right.

It was without doubt a very clean little hospital, but it was busy. There were staff everywhere, their seniority apparently determined by a variety of coloured tunics.

The sick and needy were certainly not neglected in the care department. And just in case, each and every patient seemed to have at least five family members in tow, mostly female.

Justin and Trudy sat and waited opposite two family groups, some of whom were wailing in grief.

Justin amused himself trying to decide whether their anguish was real or imagined.

There was a woman dressed in Western clothes with a bright yellow scarf wrapped around her hair. Justin judged her to be in her thirties. She was weeping gently into a handkerchief.

'That's real,' he judged.

He pretended the fact she was extremely attractive wasn't clouding his judgement.

An elderly Muslim woman dressed head to toe in black and rocking on her heels wailed out loud for all to hear.

'Too dramatic,' he decided. 'Fakin' it.'

He looked at Trudy again.

He smiled, trying to show all was forgiven. To portray, no matter how preposterous her accusations in the taxi, they were friends again now. She had actually been screaming at him inches from his face. Calling him some terrible things.

'Where did that come from?' he wondered again.

Still, all was forgotten now.

'Well, not exactly forgotten,' he conceded. 'More put on the list with all the other bitter recriminations and buried deep.'

They looked away from each other.

Justin returned to his game of genuine grief or drama queen. Intermittently he would glance towards Trudy.

'At least she's not crying,' he thought.

He didn't dwell on the fact that 'at least she's not crying' wasn't exactly the mark of a memorable vacation.

'At least the hospitals nice,' he told himself and clung to that fact as though it were a good thing. Something he'd tell people when talking about the trip.

Finally, Megan appeared. A young man in a white tunic was wheeling her towards them. A woman in a blue tunic walked alongside, holding Megan's hand.

The giant scratch had been painted with iodine so was now black and impossible to miss. Megan wore a giant sticker of a beaming cartoon frog. It covered her whole chest.

"Look, Mummy, I got a bravery sticker," she announced proudly as they drew level.

"That's nice, darling," Trudy replied.

"You are the parents?" the nurse was addressing Justin.

He felt he should explain. "Well, no, I'm not her father, but yes sort of, she's with us, you know how it is these days."

The nurse frowned at him, puzzled.

"I'm her mother," Trudy interjected.

CHAPTER TWENTY-FIVE

"What shall we do today?" Justin asked at breakfast.

"You heard the nurse, Megan has to rest."

"I'll be downstairs." Philip preferred the reception area where he could get a guaranteed wi-fi signal.

"I'll go for a walk then," Justin said.

"Fine."

He strolled through the narrow streets of Marrakech until he found what he was looking for —

"Hashish!"

The word was hissed at him. His ears pricked up. He stopped and allowed the whisperer to catch up.

"How much?" Justin asked.

Soon he was back on the rooftop. He had an ice-cold litre of water. He had two chocolate bars labeled in Arabic but looking suspiciously like a Mars bar and a Twix. And he had a lump of hash so soft he could roll it into a joint without even heating it up.

The terrace was empty. He sat down with a sigh. If he was honest, it was nice to get a bit of time to himself.

Who knew travelling with kids could be so stressful? Who

knew you had to watch little ones constantly? He wondered how parents ever managed to enjoy a life of their own.

But he took solace where he could. Trudy's lack of enthusiasm regarding their sex life was obviously nothing to do with him and everything to do with the fact that she was always babysitting.

He blew a huge cloud of smoke over the city and vowed to help her with that.

CHAPTER TWENTY-SIX

Megan recovered remarkably quickly.

They were on the terrace eating breakfast together when Justin suggested Trudy take some time off.

She stared at him, "Excuse me?"

"You can stay here and relax," he said. "You've had a tough few days."

She was taken a little by surprise.

"Are you serious?"

"Of course. Why not? You know, share the burden of responsibility. I'm a grown-up to you know."

"Well, yes, I know. If you're sure?"

"Of course I'm sure," he said, choosing to ignore her concerned expression. "I'll take her for a wander. " He turned to Megan.

"It'll be fun, won't it?"

"Will there be tortoises?" she asked.

"Yes, I expect so."

"I wanna go with him," Megan declared.

"You comin', Philip?" Justin ventured.

The teenager shrugged without looking up from his phone. Justin took that as a "yes."

"So that's settled then." He smiled at Trudy.

"Ok," she agreed, without seeming as grateful as he'd supposed she must be.

'How hard can it be? She needs to have a bit more faith,' he thought.

Justin was determined not to mess up. Once Megan had been smothered in sun cream, off they went together. The three amigos out onto the busy streets of Marrakech.

"We'll go to the square, shall we?" he suggested. "Maybe grab a coffee?"

Megan gave him a look. "I don't drink coffee, silly," she replied.

"Have you ever tried it?"

"No," she admitted.

She'd always assumed she was too young for coffee. He seemed to be implying that was not the case. She was intrigued.

"I suppose we could have a coffee," she decided.

Megan was feeling very grown-up. Obviously being so mature she didn't need to be holding his hand. She wriggled free so softly, he didn't even notice.

"What about there?" she pointed at a cafe on the edge of the square.

Justin smiled and headed towards it.

There was an empty table on the wide veranda that they all flopped down at.

"This'll do, eh?" Justin said.

Megan took in the surroundings, feeling very grown up.

"Yes," she agreed. "This'll do."

"Alright, Philip?" Justin asked.

He grunted without looking up. Justin took that as a "yes."

"So what shall we do afterwards?" he asked Megan.

"See the tortoises," she shot back.

He smiled as the waiter approached. Justin didn't see what all the fuss was about. Looking after children was easy.

"Sir?" The waiter pulled out his notepad and pen. He prepared to take their order.

"Coffee!" Megan said loudly.

"Please," Justin told her. "Don't forget to say please."

"Please," she added.

The waiter wagged his finger at her. He pursed his lips. He appeared concerned.

"No coffee," he said.

"Please."

"Sorry, no coffee."

She stared at him for a split second, and then banged her little fist down on the table.

"Coffee!" she screamed. "I want coffee!"

"It's ok." Justin had to raise his voice to be heard. "She's allowed," he added by way of explanation.

"Tea?" the waiter seemed to be suggesting instead.

"Coffee!" she replied, more loudly.

Then it became the same word repeatedly in time with banging on the table.

"Coffee, coffee, coffee."

It turned out they didn't sell coffee in that particular establishment. Nor in the next three they tried. They all sold mint tea. They all tried to make the little girl stop crying. They all made her worse.

'I could just leave her,' Justin thought, *'just for a minute to sort my head out. She'd be easy to find again. Just follow the sound of her screams.'*

He was reassessing the ease of parenthood when something cut through his thoughts. Something was wrong. He scanned his surroundings, looking for something out of place.

Then it struck him that the screaming had ceased.

'The screaming's stopped. That's what's different.'

He was midway through congratulating himself when it suddenly occurred he couldn't see her either.

He scanned the crowds.

"Philip!" he barked, and his voice had something about it that made the teenager look. "Where's your sister?"

Philip shrugged and returned his attention to his phone.

"Megan!" Justin screamed.

At the sound of her name, she rose to her feet. She had been crouched down inspecting a small cage of tortoises. Hidden behind the legs of the throngs of people.

"Look," she said, wide-eyed with excitement. "How many can we have?"

Justin had turned white. Losing her, then finding her again, so soon and so close, and so obviously unharmed played havoc with his nerves.

"Look," she said again, oblivious to his torment.

The tortoises were about two inches long. Megan had three of them crawling in a line up her arm. She was trying to hide a fourth up her sleeve.

Justin took a deep breath. He composed himself. He crouched down to Megan's level and smiled, hoping to convey calmness.

"One," he said. "You can have one."

"That's not fair."

He extracted the one from her sleeve and gave it to the vendor.

"It is fair."

He rose to his feet and pulled his wallet out.

"How much for one?" he asked the man.

"Six hundred dirham." The man smiled at him.

"What?" Justin was shocked.

He did a quick calculation.

'I could buy an ounce of hash for that.'

"No, really." He smiled to show he was in on the joke. "How much?"

"Six hundred," the man repeated, holding out his hand.

It felt a lot like daylight robbery, but he paid up.

"Come on," he said. "Hold my hand."

"I can't," Megan objected.

He was about to give her a lecture on little girls who run off and end up getting sold into the white slave trade.

"I have to take care of Justin." She held up the tiny reptile.

"I've named him after you, cos you paid for him." She smiled and stroked its shell.

Justin glanced down at it, crawling along her arm.

"It looks like it's trying to get away," he said.

Megan frowned.

"He's not an it, he's a he," she said in a tone that left no room for argument. "An' he loves me." She sounded adamant about that too. "I'm going to take him back home on the aeroplane," she announced.

Justin smiled nervously in response. He hadn't thought of that. Before he could think of a reply, a random stranger approached them.

"Tannery?" he whispered.

"Pardon?" Justin replied.

The stranger tipped his fez at Megan.

"Hello, pretty girl," he smiled.

"Hello," she replied. "I've got a tortoise." She stopped and held it out for inspection, and the man took it.

"Does he want to see where we take the goats?"

Megan nodded enthusiastically.

He stroked the animal's shell as he walked away.

"It's down here," he announced over his shoulder.

"What is?" Justin wanted to know.

"The tannery," came the over the shoulder reply.

"What?"

"The tannery," Megan repeated as though she were the adult and he the child. "What's the tannery?" she asked her new friend.

"It's where we take the goats," he replied.

"Oh, are you allowed tortoises there?" she asked.

"Of course," he reassured her.

The smell was overwhelming. They were given a little sprig of lavender to hold to their noses, but it did nothing to stop the foul stench of rotting flesh filling their nostrils.

Justin was explaining that they didn't really need to see goat decomposing. And he certainly didn't intend paying for the privilege, no matter how much the guide thrust his hand out.

Then he turned around, and Megan was gone.

The knot of dread reappeared in his stomach. He called her name and frantically began skirting the site.

"Mister!" he heard the call and raced to the worker who was pointing.

Megan's straw hat was floating in a vat of brown, smelly sludge.

"Oh shit," he exclaimed.

Workers were already rushing over with long poles and swirling them through the water.

'Like they might snag a body,' Justin thought.

"Oh shit," he said again.

"Megan!" he called.

"What?" she answered.

He spun round and there she was. Perched on the end of a stone bench, hidden by the crouching bulk of her brother.

Justin could have wept with joy, but he felt the situation demanded some marking.

"I told you to keep hold of my hand," he said, and the child looked at him mystified from around her brother.

"What happened to your hat?" he tried instead.

"I took it off," she replied.

"Mister, you want?"

A worker interrupted. He was holding a soggy, misshapen hat on the end of a pole.

"Yuck," Megan said.

"No, thanks," Justin said.

"Can we go now?" Philip said, and they both looked at him.

Justin knew when he was defeated. Parenting was much harder than he'd imagined. He was exhausted already. He needed a break.

It was time to drop the kids back. Sneak off to get stoned and read his book. Nobody could say he hadn't done his bit for the cause. Trudy was bound to appreciate the gesture.

She was getting some quality time you might say. He glanced at his watch.

'An hour and twenty minutes! Bloody Hell! It seems much longer.'

"Yeah," he said. "Let's go back."

CHAPTER TWENTY-SEVEN

They climbed the staircase to see Trudy sitting at the iron table. She was still in her dressing gown, a towel wrapped round her head.

"Oh." She seemed a little surprised to see them. "You're back already."

Megan rushed towards her and threw herself onto her mother's lap. "I got a tortoise, Mummy, look!" She thrust it into her face.

Trudy instinctively pulled away, and the jug of water before her went flying.

Philip had slumped down on the cushions. It was impressive the way he wriggled to the edge so as not to get wet, without really looking up from his screen.

"Want me to get a towel?" Justin asked.

Megan was wailing in delight, swinging on her mum, keeping her feet high. Trudy was trying to defend her more delicate regions from the flying feet. She spared Justin a withering glance.

"I'll get a towel," he decided for her and turned on his heel.

"Ask if they've sorted the hot water," Trudy called disapprovingly as he vanished down the staircase.

He went to the ground floor and called out, "Hello." Nobody came.

He wandered through to the back of the property where an ancient Moroccan man came into view in the shadow of a marble pillar.

Justin asked if there was anyone about. The man stared at him blankly.

He asked for a towel. Nothing but a blank stare.

He mimicked drying his hands. The old man looked at him until Justin felt ridiculous. Defeated Justin climbed the stairs, one weary step at a time.

He came out onto the flat roof where his eyes took in white fluffy towels spread over the spilt water. The crisis was under control. Justin glanced about him.

Philip was on his phone.

Megan was lying on the floor with Malik, trying to make her tortoise swim in the last remnants of the puddle. Any crisis was long gone.

"What did they say about the hot water?" asked Trudy.

He had to admit to himself she didn't look the happiest he'd ever seen her.

"There was nobody there." He saw her jaw harden.

"Won't he know?" he gestured at Malik.

"Hey," Justin said, and the child looked up. "Follow me."

Malik rose to his feet; Megan followed suit.

Justin led the way into the bathroom. Malik and Megan stood respectfully as Justin asked about the workings of the plumbing system.

It was adorable how both children listened attentively.

The boy because he wanted, above all, to please the funny English people, Megan because she was faithfully copying her little chum. It made her feel all grown up.

And Justin tried, he really did.

He used non-technical words and phrases from the start. Reduced them further and further until he was just running the hot tap and repeating the words, "No hot. Boiler?"

Megan got what he was saying. She didn't know why or where the boiler was. Or even what a boiler might conceivably do. But she was pleased to be following this obviously adult conversation. Megan nodded seriously.

The boy alongside her caught the movement; he nodded too, repeatedly. "Yess," he said.

He looked at Justin, wrung his hands, shook his head, nodded, said "Yess" a few times and waited.

It was a stalemate. Justin waited too; they looked each other in the eye.

To Megan's delight, the child repeated his process.

It did eventually dawn on Justin that he was going to crack first.

"Ok." He stood up. "When?" he asked, tapping an imaginary watch.

"Yess," came the reply.

He couldn't take it anymore. He walked away and left them to it.

"Well?" Trudy asked.

She was standing in the middle of the courtyard, looking at him through dark shades. The powerful sun skimmed the rooftops and backlit her perfectly. Justin was too defeated to stare. She knew something must be wrong.

He walked closer.

"He said they'll fix it while we're out."

"Out?" she said. "Where to?"

"Let's hire a taxi, go up into the mountains," he suggested.

She twitched her nose.

"Or to the coast?"

She sort of smiled. "Ok," she said.

Soon they were bumping across a hard track heading for the Atlantic coast. The driver would be paid when they arrived. Then presumably paid again when he dropped them back this evening. He'd been a little vague on detail, but no matter, they were on their way to the beach, they were in high spirits, and the sun was shining. Surely that was what mattered.

Soon the high spirits were wearing a little thin. Sometime after that, even Justin wasn't sure he could take much more. Silence had long since descended inside the baking vehicle; even Megan was subdued.

Just when Justin was idly wondering whom amongst them would break down in tears first – he'd definitely not ruled himself out – the driver broke the silence.

"Da," he said, pointing forwards.

There it was, the Ocean.

At the crest of the next hill, he pointed again and they saw a beautiful golden beach sweeping majestically away in both directions.

Smiles began to appear on the faces of the four passengers. Nobody had the strength to engage in conversation, but they certainly began to perk up.

"Da," the driver said again. This seemed to be the word he used for all foreigners, to explain all things.

He parked, climbed from the driver's seat, removed their bags from the trunk, and stood beaming like an indulgent grandfather as, one by one his passengers exited and admired the glorious beach before them.

Then he was standing before Justin with his hand out.

"Da," he said, looking shifty.

Justin thought all people wanting money looked shifty. He didn't make anything of it.

"Yes, yes, of course." He pulled out his wallet and peeled off the agreed sum. The man's hand lingered a moment, so he added another note.

The driver beamed. He shook Justin's hand enthusiastically, waved to the others individually, climbed behind his wheel and drove off.

They stood, watching him go smiling.

Slowly the smiles faded. Before long they'd all realised, even Megan, that they had effectively been abandoned in the middle of nowhere.

'Well, not in the middle because we're by the sea. On the edge of nowhere then,' Justin conceded privately as he looked towards Trudy.

"Lovely beach innit?" he beamed.

She stared at him.

He stared back.

A stray curl blew across her face in an extremely feminine manner. She looked so beautiful, he felt an overwhelming urge to kiss her.

He decided against it, at least for the time being.

"Where is everybody?" Philip asked, and they stared at him as they always did when he spoke.

"Here they are!" Megan exclaimed excitedly.

They all turned to look the way she was pointing and there they were.

A man in a full-length tunic trailed by children.

They watched the little group approach, so missed others coming at them from the far end of the beach and across the dunes.

In a few minutes, they were surrounded. A smattering of grown men and at least fifteen children mainly dressed in Nike or Adidas or Disney T-shirts.

The men hung back as the children circled around Justin. They all had their hands out, hoping for money or sweets or god knows what.

Justin stood his ground as the kids jabbered away at him. He kept repeating in unashamed English, "We ain't got any." He was smiling but obviously adamant.

The kids soon gave up. Then they were playing tag with Megan as though they'd known each other all their lives.

Eventually, a man with a smattering of English was brought forward. "You like our beach?"

"Yes, very much. It's very nice."

"You have food?"

Justin swivelled his head towards Trudy.

"Some," she said.

"We have food together," said the man.

He called one of the children over and jabbered away at him in Arabic. The boy went racing off.

He returned half-an-hour later with more men, another small army of children, and a steel drum. Fish was produced and a fire started. The drum became a grill; giant tomatoes and onions were added.

They ate dinner watching the African sun slip into the sea. It was truly idyllic, romantic even.

Trudy sat on the rug provided and watched her children.

She could see Philip a little way down the beach. He was hidden under his hood, absorbed by his phone, so he was fine.

She watched Megan racing up a sand dune with an army of children. They were all hollering and laughing, so she was fine.

She looked across at Justin and had to admit this was nice.

He glanced up at her, and she deigned to throw him a smile.

Justin was trying to think of something romantic to say when the English speaker appeared at his side. He explained that for a reasonable price, sleeping arrangements could be made, and somebody would drive them back to Marrakech tomorrow.

"Hashish?" Justin asked.

A bit of hash was added, and the deal was agreed.

As darkness fell, a giant Bedouin canopy was erected on the sand. A fire had been lit, and the sky contained a thousand stars. Trudy cuddled up to Justin in front of the flames.

'This is actually dead romantic,' she thought.

'You can't fight destiny,' he thought.

CHAPTER TWENTY-EIGHT

J ustin awoke to the sound of children laughing.

They were also pulling at his blanket. He scared them off with a growl. He stretched and saw Trudy further down the beach staring out to sea. She was sipping a mint tea. He made a joint and went to join her. Tea was poured for him, and before he'd even half-finished it, the English speaker appeared out of nowhere and came to Justin's side.

"My cousin can take you back," he said.

"Great."

Trudy smiled.

"But not yet."

The smile left her face.

"When?" Justin asked.

"When he is driving tourist bus. We can go meet him. He will take you. You will be in Marrakech tonight."

"Ok," Trudy said, and they both looked at her, waiting for her to elaborate. "We can have a day here." She was happy enough. "A day at the seaside," she added.

"Yeah," Justin agreed.

Megan was in her element, running free with a pack of

kids; Philip was content to live in the virtual world he carried with him. He was never difficult to please. Trudy lay on the sand sunbathing, relaxing while Justin sat alongside her like a lovesick puppy dog. They took a couple of swims together in the ocean, and the locals provided more food.

It was a memorable day, but by the time the sun was waxing in the sky, Trudy, in particular, was ready to leave.

Two hours later, they actually left.

The driver made them wait, but when he finally turned up, he put their minds at ease. The car was newish, clean and tidy, and once they set off, the man himself proved to be that rare thing in Morocco, a safe driver.

"We'll take the road across the Atlas Mountains," he told them. "We'll see the lights of Marrakech in three hours."

Megan had enjoyed a hectic day. She tried to fight sleep, but with the added motion of the wheels, she was soon out for the count, and peace fell upon them all.

One hour later they hit a police roadblock.

Everyone was bundled out of the vehicle. As soon as she made contact with the cold mountain air, Megan was wide-awake and screaming the place down.

Justin thought the police looked about to beat her into submission at one point.

The car driver was treated with extreme suspicion. It was almost as though the police knew him.

Then the supposed father of the screaming child was singled out for questioning.

"Where are you going?"

"Marrakech."

"Where have you been?"

"To the coast, I don't know the name of the place. He'll tell you." He pointed at their driver.

The policeman stared in suspicious silence for a moment.

Justin felt deeply concerned they would find the lump of dope he had hidden in his shoe.

"Show me your bag."

Fortunately, the police satisfied themselves with emptying his bag and patting him down.

"You want to go?" Justin was asked.

He nodded hopefully.

"One hundred dirham," said the cop in heavily accented English. It was as though he knew there was something going on; he just couldn't be bothered to carry out a thorough search.

Justin's stress levels were off the scale; he paid up gladly.

'God, I need a spliff,' he thought.

They were allowed to continue on their journey.

Megan treated them all to a nonsensical song about camels. It had fifty-seven very similar verses.

CHAPTER TWENTY-NINE

I t was the last day of the holiday.

After breakfast on the terrace, they strolled around the square for a final time, taking photographs, browsing the items for sale, pretending they were normal.

"Look," Megan said, "snakes! Let's see the snakes."

Nobody moved fast enough for her liking, so she grabbed her mother's hand and began to drag. "Come on, Mummy."

More wary than curious of the cobras, Justin followed yet stayed firmly in the background.

"Why are they here, Mummy?"

"So people can have a photo taken with them."

"Oh." She seemed satisfied with the answer.

"Do you want a photo with the python?" Justin asked.

"Yes, please," she replied, far too quickly for her mother's liking.

"Are you sure, darlin'? They can bite."

"No, no lady, no bite" assured the snake man who'd approached them and been listening attentively.

"They don't bite?" asked Megan.

"No, little lady."

Trudy threw Justin a look, which he completely misinterpreted. *'Now see what you've done,'* it said.

He read it as, *'What about Philip?'*

"What if your brother goes first?" Justin proposed.

Megan nodded enthusiastically at the suggestion. She went behind her brother and began pushing him forward.

"Get off," he grumbled, but he'd covered the short distance without realising what was going on. Now he was on the spot, in position.

"Gonna show your sister how it's done?" Justin asked.

"How what's done?"

He'd been on his phone. He hadn't been following the conversation, hadn't even noticed the snakes. He was desperately trying to get up to speed.

At this point, a python was slung round his neck.

It was a large heavy animal.

The teenager wasn't expecting to suddenly be wearing a giant snake. He staggered slightly, took a couple of steps backwards and did a sort of funny dance. He wanted to push the creature off but didn't have a clue what the correct protocol was. He didn't want to get bitten, something he was genuinely concerned by because the snake's searching tongue was practically licking his eye. The expression on his face as he tried to look at something so close was priceless, unique, the bug-eyed madness of somebody who wished they could run away from a part of themselves.

He should never have stepped so close to the cobra on the floor. But then he could hardly be held responsible; he didn't know it was there. Naturally, the animal reacted to protect itself.

Philip screamed, "I've been bitten!"

"No," the snake owner reassured him.

"There's blood on my leg."

"No."

"There's blood on his leg, he's been poisoned," insisted Trudy, sounding a little frantic.

"No blood, no poison," said the snake guy, denying the existence of blood they could all see, thereby casting doubt on whether they should believe him about the poison.

"I read somewhere they take the poison out of them," Justin offered up, trying to be helpful.

"Is he going to die?" asked Megan.

"Where did you read that?" Trudy wanted to know.

"Er," he felt pressured, "I don't remember, somewhere."

"Well, that's a lot of fuckin' good," she hissed.

"Let's take him to the Hospital?" suggested Justin, feeling a bit misunderstood.

Fortunately, there were taxis parked on the square so getting to the hospital was a straightforward operation. Once there, they were seen almost immediately. It was a professionally conducted experience that put Trudy's mind greatly at ease.

The doctor reassured her that snakes in the square did have their venom sacks removed. So Philip needed it cleaned, a tetanus jab, and he was good to go.

They would still make their flight.

CHAPTER THIRTY

Back on the terrace, Justin sat at the iron table making a joint. He had already thrown his few belongings into his bag and was waiting for the others to finish packing. He was trying to smoke all his dope. He didn't want to leave any behind; it would have felt like some kind of mini defeat. So there were great clouds of smoke drifting lazily above his head. He was like a man possessed, making joints before even finishing the one he was smoking.

In her room, Trudy braced herself. She fixed a smile in place and stepped through the doorway onto the terrace. Justin looked up immediately and grinned as she approached.

"All finished are we?"

"Almost," she said and came round the table until she was facing him.

She leant forward, rested her hands on the back of a chair, then, changing her mind, stood up straight and folded her arms. She seemed a little tense.

"Are you alright?" Justin asked.

"Fine," she said.

And he accepted her answer at face value.

He looked down. Began to stick some rizla papers together.

Trudy leant forward again, causing him to look up.

"The thing is," she said, "there's no easy way to say this."

"What?" he interrupted.

"Well, if you let me finish, I'll tell you."

"Tell me what?"

"I want you to get a different flight." She blurted the words out and took the joint from him at the same time.

He watched her take a few puffs whilst his brain somersaulted inside his skull.

"What?" he sounded shocked.

"You heard."

"Why?"

"You know why."

"I don't."

She stood before him, looking amazing, smoking his dope. She was waiting for him to agree. She passed him back his joint, and he took it, stunned into silence.

"Well?" she asked.

"Are you joking?" he wanted to check.

"No."

"You're serious?"

"Yes, I'm serious. I'd really appreciate it if you would do this because it's important to me."

'Surely she's not saying she doesn't want to be on the same plane as me,' he thought.

"There are other flights to London," she added.

"Yeah, there are, er, ok, I guess so."

And there was her little half-smile again.

"I thought we had something special," Justin said.

She had turned away but stopped and turned back when he spoke. She looked him up and down. "We don't," she said.

"But I'm only just getting to know you, discover your hidden depths," he insisted.

"There are no hidden depths to you," she replied.

She was making him feel not offended exactly, but as though he ought to be offended.

"What's wrong with that?" he wanted to know.

Trudy sighed. "You don't want to know."

"I do." He didn't really; he was just prolonging her leaving.

"Nothin', I suppose," she paused "As long as your attributes are worthy and selfless."

The silence grew awkward. Like he was expected to respond, but he didn't have anything.

'Did she just call me selfish?' He wasn't absolutely certain, but it sounded like it.

Trudy spoke, "Yours aren't. Your attributes, they're not worthy."

"Or selfless. Yeah, thanks, I got that." Finally, he was showing genuine emotion; he sounded hurt.

"Justin you are the only person I know who is exactly what they appear to be."

He perked up a bit. "Thanks," he said, "that means a lot to me."

"It's not a compliment, it's unbearable!"

"What?" He was confused again.

'This is some kind of joke,' he thought. *'She's gone mental.'*

She seemed embarrassed. Couldn't catch his eye.

"We work better in London, don't we?" he said. "Everything will be fine when we get back, eh?" He was smiling.

Trudy sighed. *'He genuinely hasn't got a clue,'* she realised.

"Look," she said, "don't take this personally, but you represent everything I hate in life."

'Don't take it personally?' he thought. *'Ouch'*

"Oh," he said.

He was floundering now. Reality could be harsh when it crashed into you with great force.

'So we're splitting up?' his addled brain was having a real problem analysing so much unexpected information.

Trudy looked him up and down shaking her head. "You're not a kid anymore," she told him. "Grow up."

'What is her problem?' He was offended by that last remark.

"So, we're splitting up?" he asked again.

"We are," she said it rather calmly, all things considered, he thought. "And if you ever try to contact me, I'll put a restraining order on you," she added.

"Oh," he said, instantly ditching his plan to leave it a week before calling her.

There didn't seem to be anything to add. But the silence made Justin uncomfortable, it was awkward, he had to say something before she disappeared.

"Have a nice life."

"Huh," she replied, turning away.

CHAPTER THIRTY-ONE

Justin looked over the street from the rooftop terrace with a fat joint in his mouth.

He could see Trudy below wheeling the suitcase. Megan was a couple of steps behind dragging her bunny by the ears, and Philip was bringing up the rear, absorbed by his phone. None of them looked up.

He watched them get in a taxi and drive away.

'Not sure where I went wrong,' he mused. *'But at least I can look myself in the mirror and say I tried, I really tried.'*

He flicked his roach across the rooftops and sat down to make another joint.

His flight wasn't until midnight. He'd bought another big lump of hash and was determined to smoke it, therefore ensuring he got on the plane stoned.

'Girls are weird,' he thought to himself. *'There's nothing I can do about that; there's nothin' anyone can do about it. It's nobody's fault, just one of those things like snow in summer or rain when you least need it.'*

· · ·

Trudy sat in the back of the taxicab. She felt a giant weight lifting from her shoulders. The lines in her face disappeared, the furrow in her brow softened the further the distance from Justin.

"It'll be wonderful to get home, won't it?" she mused out loud.

She wondered if she should apologise yet beg forgiveness for subjecting them both to such a traumatic experience.

And if any good at all was to come from this disaster, it was going to be that from now on she was determined to be a better mother.

"I don't want to go home. I wanna stay," said Megan.

"Excuse me," her mother was surprised to hear that.

"I love Morocco," Megan added. "I never want to leave."

Trudy stared at her, aghast.

"Wow," she said.

"Stop the car," Megan was suddenly dishing out orders.

"No, No, sssh. The man's taking us to the airport."

"Can't we stay here?"

"No, dear, I'm sorry we can't. But we can perhaps come back one day. Would that be nice?"

"I love it here," Megan replied.

"That's lovely, dear, I'm glad."

"We'll come back one day," Megan answered happily.

"Philip?" Trudy was interested in her son's opinion.

He didn't answer. She had to tug his sleeve to get his attention. He removed the headphones hidden by his hood.

"What?" he asked.

"I'm sorry it was such a mess," she said.

"Huh, what was?"

"You know, the trip, Justin, the whole thing."

"Who's Justin?" he replied.

THE END

Dear reader,

We hope you enjoyed reading *Make or Break In Marrakesh*. Please take a moment to leave a review, even if it's a short one. Your opinion is important to us.

Discover more books by Ian Parson at

https://www.nextchapter.pub/authors/ian-parson

Want to know when one of our books is free or discounted? Join the newsletter at http://eepurl.com/bqqB3H

Best regards,

Ian Parson and the Next Chapter Team

ABOUT THE AUTHOR

Ian Parson was born in Plymouth. He has travelled extensively and lived in London, Spain & Greece. His first novel *A Secret Step* (Copperjob) was published in 2013. In 2014 he provided the opening chapter for *The Little Book of Jack the Ripper* (HistoryPress).

His second novel *The East End Beckons* (Linkville) was published in 2015.

Both novels were critically acclaimed.

In 2016 he provided the opening chapter for *A Linkville New Year* (Linkville).

His third novel *The Grind* (Next Chapter) was published in 2019

He has had numerous articles published in Spain and the UK.

Ian has a keen interest in the history of London and is an active member of the Whitechapel Society and the Orwell Society.

Make Or Break In Marrakesh
ISBN: 978-4-86747-759-5

Published by
Next Chapter
1-60-20 Minami-Otsuka
170-0005 Toshima-Ku, Tokyo
+818035793528

22nd September 2021

9 784867 477595